Wait and See

Wait and See

Virginia Bradley

COBBLEHILL BOOKS

Dutton / New York

Library of Congress Cataloging-in-Publication Data
Bradley, Virginia, date
Wait and see / Virginia Bradley.
p.   cm.
Summary: Eleven-year-old Amy faces big changes in her world, as the
woman who has cared for her and her grandfather most of her life
prepares to move back to England and an unusual new girl appears
in her classroom at school.
ISBN 0-525-65158-6
[1. Orphans—Fiction.   2. Friendship—Fiction.]   I. Title.
PZ7.B7259Wai 1994   [Fic]—dc20   93-27474   CIP   AC

Published in the United States by Cobblehill Books,
an affiliate of Dutton Children's Books,
a division of Penguin Books USA Inc.,
375 Hudson Street, New York, New York 10014
Designed by Joy Taylor
Printed in the United States of America
First Edition   10 9 8 7 6 5 4 3 2 1

To my son, Stephen,
the first to remind me
I was still part child.

Wait and See

I

BY THE TIME they got around to telling me, it was all settled. Doff was leaving, going back to England to take care of her mother, and the Judge and I would have to get someone else to look after us.

It was Sunday night, and we were still sitting around the dining room table with the empty pudding dishes. The Judge tapped his fingers together the way he does when he expects me to explode. And I sure did.

"How come I didn't know this was happening, Grandpa?" I almost shouted. "Why didn't somebody talk to me about it?"

Doff put her hand on mine. "I'm sorry, Luv, but don't blame the Judge. I got the call only this afternoon—late. Poor Mum hasn't been doing well since she broke her hip last month, and the doctor says she just can't live alone anymore. Besides, no matter how much we were to talk, there isn't anything else I can do but go to her."

"There's got to be something. You can't just all at once fly off across the ocean and leave us. It isn't fair."

"Of course it isn't, but it's one of those things we have to accept. I'll be here awhile yet, and the Judge will find someone to look after you—someone you'll like."

"I won't like anybody. I only want you." I looked over at the Judge. "You tell her, Grandpa."

But there wasn't any help on the Judge's face and less from his mouth. "She's free to do whatever she thinks she should, Amy." He cleared his throat. "If that means leaving us to go to her mother, I understand."

"Well, I don't." I could feel my face getting hot. "You can't go, Doff. You belong to us."

"You think I haven't thought about all the wonderful years we've had together? You were only two when I came, and now here you are eleven." She gave me that lopsided smile of hers. "But I also belong to Mum, and if I'm not there, they'll just bundle her off to some home. You wouldn't want that to happen to her now, would you, Luv?"

I didn't answer. What did I know about mothers? Doff was the closest I had. There was a big picture of my father on the mantel, his high school graduation picture, but I had only snapshots of my mother. Anyhow, I never knew either one of them. They were both dead, and there was just Doff and the Judge as far back as I can remember.

My eyes were wet, and I ran out into the hall and upstairs, just to get away.

Safe in my room, I plopped down on the bed and stared at

the ceiling. I wasn't going to cry. I'm the one who always says if you've got a problem to work out, tears are a waste of time.

The Judge was right. We couldn't tell Doff what to do. She wasn't blood family, even if she did make sure I knew her taking care of me was a happy thing.

"You were too little to remember," she used to say, "but we hit it off right from the start." Then she'd wink. "Probably because that first day you found the tea biscuits in my pocket."

I think I do remember though. If I close my eyes tight I can just see this lady holding out her hands to me, a lady with pink cheeks who smelled like flowers.

Sure she wasn't my mother, but she did belong to me. I hated that broken-boned Mum who lived off in England and wanted to take her away.

I don't know how long I was there on the bed just using up time, but it was dark in the room when I heard the heavy knock on the door. The Judge.

I wasn't surprised. I knew he'd come. I sat up, rubbed my hand over my eyes, and he knocked again.

"Come on, Amy," he said. "Come on downstairs and we'll talk this over."

"I don't want to, Grandpa." I snapped on the light and looked at my clock. It was eight-thirty. "I'm going to read awhile. Then I'm going to bed."

"But, Amy, we have to be practical."

"Please. Just go away." I heard him sigh and go back downstairs. I was still mad, but I was sorry too. I didn't want to make him feel bad.

The Judge isn't a "climb-in-my-lap" kind of grandpa, but I know he loves me and he's a great man. Just ask anybody in

3

town. Ask Jessie. Just go down to her coffee shop next to the bus station and ask her. She'll tell you how super he is, always helping somebody. Besides, I've seen him at the courthouse myself. He has answers for everyone—except maybe for me. Doff's the one who gives me answers—up to now anyhow. She was the one who told me the Judge was kind of an orphan himself. Grandma Ryker died before I was even born. He did have a housekeeper, but after my mother and father were killed and I was dumped on him because he was the only one there was, she left. Said she was no nursemaid. I guess there were nursemaids after that, maybe two or three. Then Doff.

I reached under my pillow for my new mystery, the one Roger gave me. Doff would be up to see me next, as soon as she thought I'd cooled off. She'd be harder to send away, and I wanted to be busy with something.

It didn't work though. I'd barely opened the cover and there she was at the door, asking if I'd mind if she came in. I said it was okay, but she knew it really wasn't. She knows me.

"Come on, Luv," she said, not bothering to close the door behind her. "You aren't losing me. We'll write. You'll tell me all about school and your friends, and one day you'll come to England. That's something we can plan for."

Trying to be so cheerful. I didn't want to listen, but she went right on. "And wouldn't Mum be pleased? I've told her all about you."

"If she knows all about me," I said, "she knows you can't leave us." I was being rotten, but Doff didn't seem to notice.

"Oh, dear," she said, "I'm not saying any of the right things, but I just must go. Mum needs me."

"Then you should have stayed with her in the beginning. You shouldn't have come here at all."

"Oh, Amy, she didn't need me when I came to you and the Judge. We were the ones with the need. There I was, a widow, alone in America, seeking a haven, and you, so little, reaching out for loving care. Even the Judge was at a loss. It's all different now. I wish you could see that."

"Well, I can't." I turned away from her and pulled my sleep shirt out of the closet. "Please, I'd like to get ready for bed."

"All right, I'll go. But remember I'm just as sad about this as you are, and we ought to talk about it with maturity. You are growing up, you know."

She looked sad, and after she left I felt hateful. But if she wanted me to say everything was fine she had another want coming. As for talking about it, that was what the Judge said we should do. I guess they were right. But the only person I wanted to talk to was Roger, and he was up at the lake for the weekend with his folks. They wouldn't be home until late—way past midnight maybe. There wasn't anything I could do until morning.

II

MORNING. It was almost a quarter to nine when I came down-stairs. I meant to be late. The Judge was already on his way downtown, but Doff was there ready for me as soon as I set foot inside the kitchen.

"You must have overslept," she said, and there was the lopsided smile again. "I was about to come up to get you. Still, there's time for a quick bowl of oatmeal."

"No, there isn't." I said, gulping down the orange juice set out for me. I grabbed my lunch sack and headed for the door.

"Wait, Luv, don't go off like this."

"Sorry. I've got to run." I was out of the house double-quick, down the back steps and up the alley. Roger usually meets me at the corner in front of the Fletchers' house, but he wasn't there. Maybe the Enslows didn't get back last night. Or maybe Roger just hadn't waited for me. I didn't want to believe that. He's my best friend. We go way back to playpen days, and since there weren't any other kids in the neighborhood, we were pretty well glued together by the time we went to kindergarten. Sure, when Roger started soccer last year he changed a little, spends more time with Matt and Barney than he does with me. But if I have trouble I can count on him.

I hurried along Oak Street, but when I didn't see any of the other kids I decided I was later than I meant to be. I ran the last three blocks and even then I got to class only seconds before the bell.

Roger was there. He sits just across the aisle, and I said, "Thanks for waiting. Thanks a lot."

"Where were you?" he whispered. "It was getting late."

"I made it in time, didn't I?"

Miss Pritchett's voice cut off the argument. "That was the final bell, class. Let's have it quiet, please."

I hadn't expected this to be a great day, but it went completely out of control. First of all, I remembered that my social studies report was sitting on my desk at home. All those starving children of Africa. Then during the spelling test I erased a big hole in the center of my paper. *Ocasion . . . occassion . . .* Rats! The word should have been *disaster*.

I didn't get a chance to corner Roger at recess or even at lunch. There was always somebody around. But when we came back into class at one o'clock I told him I had to talk to him. "Right after school," I said.

"I've got soccer practice, Ryker." As though that ruled out everything. "Won't be through till four-thirty."

Ryker. That was another thing Roger was doing now, calling me by my last name. I think he's trying to forget I'm a girl. It doesn't bother me. He knows I can run faster than he can, and I throw a mean curveball. Anyhow, I told him I didn't care how long he practiced. I'd wait for him. We could talk on the way home. It was important.

He said okay, and I felt better. I knew the afternoon would drag, but I'd get through it somehow.

It turned out to be easier than I expected. We were barely settled in our seats when the principal marched into the room and right up to the front desk with a new girl. I couldn't see her very well. Mr. Anderberry's a tall, fat man, and she was on the far side of him. Anyhow, he said, "Miss Pritchett, I have another sixth grader for you. Violetta Mills. I'm sure you'll find a place for her." Then he sort of handed the girl over like a present and left.

Violetta, now in plain sight, looked like a present. She had pale chalky hair that swooped down low on her forehead, and her eyes were smoky blue and shaded with dark lashes about three inches long. But the big thing was that she was all done up in white ruffles and pink bows. Nobody comes to school like that. This new person looked like she was ready for trick or treat or maybe a wedding, except the dress was a little wrinkled. It was sure dumb, but I heard a low whistle from the back of the room, and Barney, who sits behind Roger, said, "Wow!"

I don't think Miss Pritchett was happy to have another kid in the class. There wasn't a place for her. The only empty seat was right in front of me. It belonged to Sukie Adams who was still out of school with a cold. She'd probably be back to-morrow. Of course, that's where Violetta landed. Miss Pritch-ett nodded toward Sukie's desk and said, "You can sit there, dear, at least for today. We'll get you settled as soon as possible."

"Thank you," said the girl in a voice so low you could hardly hear. Then, looking straight ahead of her as if she didn't know we were all staring, she pushed that white-blonde hair off her face and came down the aisle. There was another whistle or two, one I knew was from Matt even if it wasn't his usual blast. Miss Pritchett said, "Enough of that, boys. Let's get on with our work."

That's what we did, but the new girl was still the center of attention. Everybody was watching her like they expected her to rise up and float out of the room on her ruffles. I looked over at Barney a couple of times, and he was sitting there with his chin in his hands and his mouth open, just gazing at her.

For literature we're reading *The Incredible Journey*, out loud. You know, taking turns around the room. Miss Pritchett says it takes a little extra time, but it gives us a chance to hear our own voices.

I got Sukie's book out of her desk for Violetta to use and showed her where we'd left off. Not that it mattered. When it was her turn she fumbled with the pages and Miss Pritchett told her not to worry. "It really isn't fair to call on you when you're unfamiliar with the material."

How do you like that?

Linda Shotmeyer kind of snickered and whispered something to her sister. Those two always sit right close to each other. Twins have to do that I guess. They both giggled and Violetta turned to see where the sound came from. I saw her face. Absolutely no expression at all. I wondered what she was thinking.

Miss Pritchett rapped on her desk and frowned. That was the end of that. Anyhow, I read, and Kimberly Todd, and Barney and everyone in the row by the windows. We got through two chapters. Miss Pritchett said she had a film of the Canadian wilderness with its wildlife. She thought we might enjoy it as background for the story, and she asked Matt to help her with the projector.

We can't get our room really dark enough for movies, and when the time came to watch I decided to watch Violetta instead. I noticed while the reading was going on she kind of slumped forward, and now her head was leaning over to one side. I bent down pretending to pick up something from the floor and peeked around the back of the desk. *She was asleep!* Would you believe it? In the middle of the afternoon? Where did she think she was?

In the dim light, Miss Pritchett caught my eye and shook her head. She wanted me to leave her alone. Roger looked my way and grinned. What we had here was Snow White in a blonde wig. He knew, and maybe a couple of other people. But that was all. She slept through the film, didn't even move when we opened the blinds, and it was no charming prince that finally woke her up. It was the three o'clock bell.

I didn't wait around to see whether Miss Pritchett said anything to her or what she did when she left the school. At least she kept my mind off my trouble, and I poked on down to the athletic field and waited for the practice to begin.

Soccer isn't my favorite game. One thing, they won't let girls play on the boys' team and there aren't enough girls interested to have one of our own. Sukie's willing, but she's always absent for one reason or another. The Shotmeyer twins would rather

10

play tennis, and most of the others just want to watch the boys. That's okay, I guess. Some of them are worth watching. Like today when they finally got out on the field, Roger was goalie and nobody could get by him. Matt and Barney are pretty good too. They move fast and kick up a lot of dust. But if the girls ever do get a team we'll take them on. I tried to imagine Violetta out there, but it didn't work. With that dumb hair in her eyes, she wouldn't be able to see the ball, let alone kick it.

Practice didn't last as long as Roger said it would. Mr. Tompkins was in a bad mood and kept yelling at the guys to lift their feet. He finally gave up I guess, and it was only four when we were ready to head for home.

Roger started grumbling about not being in shape for Saturday's game, and I decided to wait a little before I told him what was on my mind. Anyhow, I was still thinking about old Violetta, and I said, "I don't think I like that new girl. She's weird."

Roger stopped his grumbling and climbed up on the low wall that borders the sidewalk along Oak Street. He always does that—teeters on the narrow bricks like it was a big deal. Finally, he said, "Yeah, she's different all right, but she's sure pretty. Maybe that's why you don't like her." And he grinned.

"That's dumb. Anyhow, how come you're sticking up for her?"

"I only said she was pretty. You've got to admit that."

"Sure, if you like white hair." Roger makes me so mad sometimes. "And I didn't wait all through your practice to talk about what's-her-name."

"You brought her up."

"Well, now I'm bringing her down."

"Okay, forget it. You said you wanted to talk. What's on your mind?"

I was glad he was the one to change the subject. I took a deep breath and told him about Doff.

By the time I finished, I guess he could tell I was really hurting. He jumped off the wall and came around in front of me so I had to stand still.

"Wait a minute," he said. "You mean Doff's going for good?"

"What do you think I've been telling you?"

"But she can't do that. She's practically your mother."

"But she isn't my mother. That's the whole point. And the Judge says she can do whatever she wants to—or needs to. You've got to help me, Roger."

We walked along then without saying anything for the longest time. I guess he was thinking.

"Well?" I said. "How can I make her stay?"

I wished I hadn't asked. He shook his head the way the Judge always does and said, "I don't think you can. After all, Doff really just works for you—for the Judge. Nothing can stop her from quitting."

He might as well have punched me in the stomach. We'd reached Fletchers' corner, and I felt sick. "Is that all you can say?"

Roger turned off toward his house. "I'm sorry," he said. "Honest, Ryker, I wish I knew how to help. I'll think about it, but right now the only thing I can see is if you were worse off than Doff's mother—maybe if you had some horrible disease—she might think twice about leaving you."

"Skip it," I said, and ran down the walk to the front of our house. I didn't want to go in the back way. Doff would probably be in the kitchen and I was so miserable I didn't want to see her. As it was, what I saw on our front porch didn't make me feel any better. Snow White and her ruffles.

III

"HEY," I SAID, tossing my book bag on the steps. "Are you waiting for me?"

Snow White looked up from the magazine that was spread open across her knees. "No," she said, squinting at me through the fringe of white hair. "Why?"

"I live here, that's why. You're on my porch."

"Sorry. I didn't know." Polite words but snarpy. And the voice wasn't the same one she used in school. No trouble hearing her now. She didn't get up either, just glanced over her shoulder at our living room window and said, "You sure live in a nice place."

"It's all right." I shrugged. I never thought of our house as anything special. And it's awful old—a lot older than the Enslows'.

"Look," I said, "if you aren't waiting for me, what're you doing here? Who are you waiting for?"

"My mother." She nodded toward the front door and then went back to her magazine as if she was through talking.

All kinds of people come to see the Judge. There wasn't any reason the mother of Snow White couldn't be one of them. Just the same, today was different. Way back in my mind I was afraid this all might have something to do with Doff's leaving.

"What does she want—your mother?" I could be snarpy too.

This time the girl closed the magazine over her thumb to hold her place and gave me her full attention. "Whatever it is," she said, "it hasn't anything to do with you."

I guess that was all I really needed to know. Only it was my turn to say I was sorry. "I shouldn't have asked. It's none of my business."

"That's right. And now since I've told you why I'm here, why don't you just let me alone? I know you don't like me."

She hit the right button, and I guess I looked guilty. What could I say? But she didn't wait while I thought of something.

"You don't have to pretend," she said. "I'm not blind. Nobody in that stupid sixth grade likes me."

At least there was an answer to that. "The boys do. You heard the whistles."

"Oh, the boys. Don't tell me about the boys. They always whistle. If you really want to tell me something, tell me why you don't like me."

She had me in a corner, and I kind of backed off. Then I

surprised myself and said something I sure didn't intend to say. "Roger thinks I don't like you because you're pretty."

"Forget Roger. What's your reason?"

Okay, I might as well say it. "If you want the truth, it's your clothes. They're weird. Does your mother get you up like that?"

The look she gave me was icy. "I wear what I like. I happen to like ruffles and pink ribbon. There's no law." She flipped the hair out of her eyes with a quick move of her head. "Now is there anything else about me that bothers you?"

I'd gone this far, I might as well go on. "You asked. You fell asleep this afternoon, actually fell asleep while class was going on. Yeah, that bothered me."

"Maybe I was tired." For a minute she didn't seem quite as sure of herself.

"Nobody else could get away with that, you know. And Miss Pritchett wouldn't even let me wake you up."

"Maybe she knew I was tired. You'd be dragged out too, if you'd been on a bus all night."

Now that was something I'd sure like to hear about, and a million questions popped into my head. But before I had a chance to ask any of them the front door opened with a wide swing and there was the mother. At least I supposed she was the mother. Sure didn't look like Violetta. Shorter for one thing, and her hair was dark brown and pulled back off her face and held with a barrette. Besides, she had on jeans, a baggy blue sweater, and running shoes. She looked normal. Could have been the mother of almost any kid in school. But I couldn't put her together with Snow White. They didn't match.

16

Anyhow, Mrs. Mills, if that's who she was, came over to where the girl sat and said, "Well, Letta, another goose chase."

The Judge had followed her out the door, in fact held it open for her. "Sorry I can't be more help, Mrs. Mills," he said, "but if you're going to stay on in Newton Grove, feel free to come back to see me. This is a small town, and I think you'll find it friendly."

Mrs. Mills threw her arms up as if to say, "Don't bother to feel sorry," but all she said was, "I didn't expect anything." Then, "Come on, Letta, let's get a hamburger someplace and go to the movies. Maybe it'll be something funny." She paid no attention to me at all. I don't think she even saw me.

Violetta didn't answer her mother, and she didn't say anything more to me either. She just stood up, tucked her magazine under her arm and took ahold of her mother's hand. Yeah, took her mother's hand. That seemed kind of funny. Boy, I haven't held anybody's hand for years.

The two of them went down the porch steps without looking back, and I had a crazy thought. From where I stood, if I didn't know, I wouldn't be able to tell which one was the mother.

The Judge called after them, "Remember to keep in touch." Then he turned to me. At least he saw me.

"How long have you been home, Amy? Doff was looking for you. Better see what she wants."

"Okay," I said, but after he went back inside, I just stood there watching until the blue sweater and the white dress were out of sight around the corner. And now something else was bothering me. Do you know that twice in one day, this gooney girl, this Snow White in ruffles, took my mind away from Doff? Give her credit.

IV

I STILL WASN'T in any hurry to see Doff, but I guess I couldn't put it off any longer. I found her in the kitchen scrubbing vegetables.

"I'm home," I said. "Grandpa told me you wanted to see me."

"That was an hour ago, Luv. Not too important either. It was just that the Judge's visitor had a young girl with her. About your age. I thought you could keep her company while she waited."

"She didn't want any company."

"You saw her then?"

"I saw her. Anyhow, she started to school today. My room. She's weird."

"That's an ugly word, Amy, and it's not like you to make such a judgment."

I shrugged. "Weird's weird. You saw what she had on. She came to school like that."

"Hmm." Doff set her lips together like she does. "I seem to remember a girl who insisted on wearing tennis shoes to the church service on Easter—just last year I think. Didn't we settle for 'an expression of individualism'?"

"That was different. I hated those fancy shoes you wanted me to get."

"Of course. That was different." Doff has this way of agreeing with me when she isn't. Then she smiled and said, "By the way, Sukie called. I think she was lonely. Said she'd call again after dinner. And about dinner, we're eating a little early. Get your clothes changed. Then I'd like your help with the table." She handed me half the carrot she was slicing into the saucepan on the stove. "Have a nibble, Luv, and please don't look so glum. At least for tonight I promise not to bring up our problem. Smile now."

I didn't think I could smile again, ever, but I'll say this, Doff kept her word. Besides, she must have made a deal with the Judge. He didn't say anything either. All the same, Doff's ailing mother hung over the dinner table like a creature from another world. We talked about the days getting shorter and the leaves starting to turn. Doff said the back fence ought to be painted while we still had the good September weather, and the Judge promised to have someone take care of it. No one mentioned Violetta or her mother. I was curious about Mrs. Mills's visit, but I knew better than to ask the Judge what she wanted. He keeps people's troubles to himself.

It was a long draggy dinner with lots of quiet, and I was

sure glad when we finally cleared away the dishes and Sukie called.

I have to tell you about Sukie. We've been halfway friends since fourth grade. That's when she moved to Newton Grove. Her father bought the town paper after old Mr. Felton died.

Sukie's all right, I guess, and sometimes she's a lot of fun. We both like mystery books and licorice and monster movies, but she does have an awful busy mouth. She says she plans to be the very top newswoman of the world and maybe she's practicing, but I could never trust her with my most secret secrets like I do Roger. They might wind up on the bulletin board at school.

There's something more. Sukie always knows everything, and before anybody else, which is hard to understand when she spends so much time in bed.

Tonight, though, with the news I had I was sure I was ahead of her. I'd give it a little buildup. "Sukie," I said, "it's too bad you're always absent when stuff happens."

She stopped me with a great groan. "Amy, you know I can't help it if I'm sick, but I guess I could be dying and you wouldn't care." She coughed a little to make her point.

"Okay, I'm sorry. Don't die. At least not till you hear." And I told her about the new girl. She tried to interrupt, but I wouldn't let her. Only thing was when I got to the part about Violetta on the bus all night, Sukie seemed to get her strength back. She practically screamed at me.

"Just keep quiet for a minute, Amy Ryker. I know all that."

You see what I mean? She knows everything. And how could she?

In the next ten minutes I found out how. They were having a problem down at the paper, and her father was there most of the night.

"You know," she said, "the *Sentinel*'s right across from the bus station, and the girl you're talking about got off with her mother at five o'clock this morning. They needed a place to stay, and I guess the man at the station told them to go to the hotel, and when they didn't want that he suggested they ask at the paper. Well, they did, and Daddy sent them to Jessie's, the only other place open at that hour, and Jessie said they could have the room up over her kitchen. So that's where they're staying."

Sukie's such a gloater. I can't stand it. "Good for them," I said. "If Jessie let them stay at her place they must be all right." Sukie knows Jessie's one of my favorite people. Then I cleared my throat and asked with super control, "When did your father tell you all this?"

"At breakfast, of course." She must have remembered how sick she was supposed to be and hurried to say, "Mother told me if I felt up to it I could come downstairs to eat, and that happened to be just when Daddy came home."

I believed her all right, but this once I was sure I'd told her something she didn't know.

"At least," I said, "your father couldn't tell you about her falling asleep and about her coming to my house and . . . hey, wait a minute, what about the dress? Did he tell you about the white dress?"

There was no quick answer.

"Come on, Sukie, was she wearing the white dress?"

"I don't know." She stopped talking for a minute and then said, "Daddy doesn't pay attention to clothes. He leaves that to the fashion editor."

She always wiggles out of a tight spot, and I wanted to say something to shake her up. "Maybe your father didn't see the girl at all."

"Of course he saw her." She was rattled all right. "Daddy's the one who sent them to Jessie's. I told you that. You're just being mean." There was a fit of coughing—pretty fake but loud.

"Okay, so he saw her. But you didn't. Admit it, Sukie, you just don't know everything."

The coughing stopped. "I don't know why you're making such a big deal over this," she said. "Anyhow, I'll tell you something more. After I left the breakfast table this morning, my father thought I'd gone back upstairs, and I heard him tell Mother that this woman—he called her *this woman*—was looking for a missing husband. What do you think of that?"

"I don't think anything of that, Sukie Adams. But I do think I'm through talking with you about Violetta or whatever else." I slammed the phone down just as hard as I could.

Trouble was, I'm not sure I got the best of Sukie after all.

V

DOFF'S PROMISE not to talk about leaving sort of held over to
the next day, and Tuesday started just fine. The Judge out the
door all smiles, waffles for breakfast, and Roger waiting for
me on the corner.

Too good to last, and it didn't. Roger spoiled everything as
soon as he opened his mouth.

"I've been thinking about Doff," he said. "I told you I would,
and finally, I talked to my dad about it."

"Roger! You didn't!" I almost dropped my books. "My
troubles aren't supposed to be public property."

"What are you so hot about? I couldn't come up with any
help for you."

"So maybe you think I should put an ad in the paper."

"It was just my dad. Sometimes it doesn't hurt to ask a
grown-up. I didn't think you'd care."

"Well, I do care. You had no right to do that."

"Okay, okay. I'm sorry. It wasn't any good anyhow. Dad said Doff's mother could come here to live, but he supposed the Judge had already suggested that. Then he said the same thing I did. Oh, not about you getting a horrible disease, but that Doff could do whatever she wanted."

"I don't want to hear anymore, and thanks for nothing."

"Look, Ryker, this is a big problem—not like your lost library book or your sick cat. I'm still thinking, though. Maybe I can come up with an idea yet."

"Never mind," I said. "I'll take care of it myself." No use fighting with him. It isn't that I don't like Dr. Enslow. He's real nice and he's been my dentist as long as I've had teeth. It just made me mad to think Roger talked to him about my feelings. He'd never done that before. We'd always worked things out alone, together—the two of us.

After we turned onto Oak Street, we didn't say much, and it was like that the rest of the way. I guess we started walking faster too, because it was still pretty early when we got to school.

Roger always waits outside for Barney and some of the other boys who come from across town, but I went on into the room. Miss Pritchett was at her desk already. That didn't surprise me. Sometimes I think she sleeps there. What did surprise me was that Sukie was there too. The way she was pushing "sick" on the phone last night I'd have thought she'd be out of school for a month.

Anyhow, there she was in her regular place. I said, "Hi," and slid into my seat behind her, not noticing at first that she was busy going through all the books and papers in her desk like a detective. By the time I did notice, something else took my attention—Violetta. In she walked, same ruffled dress with the pink bows, but I swear it had been washed and maybe ironed. She was pretty, though. I had to admit Roger was right about that. It was those eyes.

I heard somebody whisper, "That dress again," but I guess Miss Pritchett didn't think it mattered what the new girl wore. She just said, "Well, dear, you do have a desk today. I had one brought in this morning. It's in the same row you were in yesterday but way at the back. I hope you don't mind. You're a tall girl, but if there's any problem let me know."

Violetta said in her school voice, "Thank you, no problem," and headed down our aisle.

I think I was going to say hello to her—really, I think I was. I mean, after all, she was staying at Jessie's. But I didn't get the chance. She stopped beside Sukie and leaned down to her. "Don't worry," she said, "I didn't take anything."

Sukie didn't look at her, just kept on flipping pages. "I'm not worried," she mumbled. "Just checking."

Miss Pritchett didn't hear any of this. More kids were coming in, gathering around her. Otherwise, I'm sure she would have said something. She's pretty fair.

Sukie was being so stupid. I tapped her on the shoulder and said, "Actually, the only thing she touched was the book we've been reading, and I got that out for her. You can blame me if there's anything wrong with it."

Sukie swung around and glared at me. "Well," she said, "aren't you just sugar? And after you were the one who told me . . ."

I didn't let her finish. "Knock it off," I said, slamming my book bag on the desk. "Just knock it off."

Violetta hadn't waited to listen. She just went to her own seat. Gave me a look, though. Only thing, I couldn't tell whether it was a "thank you" or a "mind your own business."

The rest of the day was pretty boring. Roger stayed away from me. I stayed away from Sukie, and Violetta stayed away from everybody—or tried to. The boys who whistled stopped. Instead, whenever we were out in the yard they followed her around. I don't know whether they were trying to talk to her or get her to talk to them, and I was never close enough to hear anything. I guess she was used to boys chasing after her and, I guess too, she didn't especially like it. She always seemed to duck away from them. I didn't pay much attention until I saw it was Roger who cornered her over by the drinking fountain. You know I don't ever remember Roger talking to a girl at school when he didn't have to—except for me, of course. And like I said, he hasn't been talking to me much lately. Anyhow, Violetta ducked away from him too, and I forgot about it.

When the day finally ended, Sukie's mother picked her up at the front curb. Sukie and I never walk home together anyhow. She lives across town too. Roger had practice again, and today there was absolutely no reason to wait for him. I just headed out alone. There was nothing wrong with that. I don't have too many girlfriends at school. There's never been anybody I especially wanted to hang around with. Doff keeps asking me to have someone over, to do homework, watch TV, spend the night, stuff like that. But I like being alone. Sometimes it's better.

It was funny today, though. I missed Roger, and when I saw Violetta up ahead of me, I called out to her. Don't ask why. "Hey, what's your hurry?"

She turned, tossing her hair back in that way I was getting used to. "You talking to me?"

"Yeah." I hurried to catch up with her, and as we walked along, I said, "Just want you to know I think Sukie was a real pain this morning."

"Doesn't matter." She was quick with her answer. "You don't have to protect me. Nobody does."

"I'll remember that," I said. Her look this morning was a "mind your own business" then. I guess I couldn't blame her.

She was holding her head high so that the hair stayed back off her face, and now she twisted around and looked straight at me. "You learn," she said, "when you're weird."

If she wanted to pay me back for saying what I did about her clothes, she was sure doing it. "I'll remember that too," I said. "But I'll tell you something. Doff thinks you aren't any weirder than I am."

"Doff? Who's Doff?"

To tell the truth I was sorry I'd mentioned Doff. I never had to explain her before. She was just a part of our family and everybody knew it. I kind of stammered around. "Oh, Doff's my—she's our—" Okay, if I didn't have the words I'd use Roger's, and in a very low voice, I said, "She works for us."

I felt awful saying that. But I didn't have to get so bothered. No big deal to Violetta. I don't think she even cared who Doff was. We dropped the subject, and when we got to the corner, she said, "I go this way," and pointed off toward town.

"Oh? Where do you live?" I tried to sound dumb. Remember she didn't know I knew.

"Over Jessie's coffee shop." She looked straight at me again. "My mother calls it the Upstairs Hilton."

It was like she was daring me to say something snarpy, but I didn't even blink. "Well, Jessie's is the best place in town to eat," I said. "Try her hamburgers sometime."

"We already have," she came right back at me.

And you know what? I think she smiled.

VI

I WAS TELLING the truth about Jessie's food. Her fries are the greatest. Roger and I take them to the movies instead of popcorn. Jessie's a cool person too. She runs that coffee shop practically by herself except for Ben Haggerty. He's her night cook and sometimes his wife comes in to work at the counter. Jessie's almost as old as the Judge, I think, but she doesn't look like anybody's grandmother. She wears tight jeans and a big white T-shirt that says "Jessie's Place"—a clean one every day. And then she's got this orange hair—no fooling, orange—and she pulls it up on top of her head and winds it into a kind of doughnut. Now that I think about it, if we're talking weird, I guess Jessie'd be the president of the club. Anyhow, everybody in town likes her. I sure do. She says she's partial to kids, and I go down to her place every once in awhile just to talk to her—and eat, of course. I always eat.

Doff doesn't think I ought to spend so much time at Jessie's. Oh, she likes her fine. She just says a coffee shop right next to the bus station isn't the best place for a young girl to frequent. *Frequent.* That's Doff. The Judge is on my side, though. "You worry too much," he always says. "Nobody gets out of line at Jessie's. She may be a bit flamboyant,"—isn't that a beautiful word?—"but she knows people. If you pass muster with that lady, you've got the best character witness in town."

I guess that's what I was saying to Sukie yesterday, wasn't it?

I'll tell you, though, it wasn't food I was thinking of after I left Violetta. I was wondering what it would be like living over Jessie's kitchen. I'd been up there a couple of times. Just one room and a bath. Not very big. There was a sink, a small stove and refrigerator, a table, three or four chairs. I think there was a chest of drawers or something too, but no TV and no bookshelves. I'd die there. Where would I put my mysteries and all my stuffed animals?

Violetta probably goes along with it, though. I've decided she's pretty tough. Maybe because she's with her mother. I remembered how they held hands going down our porch steps. Mothers are important, I guess. I'll bet Mrs. Mills wouldn't ever leave Violetta. I'll bet if her own mother was off in England somewhere, she'd just bring the broken-boned old lady to live with them. Sure she would.

I got to thinking about that. We could do it with Doff's mother—bring her here. That would solve everything. We had plenty of room. Roger's dad said the Judge had probably already suggested it, but maybe not. He hadn't said so. I'd find out.

When I got home Doff was on the front porch, settled into the Judge's old rocker with her knitting in her lap. I could have asked her right then, but I decided to wait. We do our serious talking at dinner. For now I just said, "Hi," and plopped down on the bottom step.

"I thought maybe you'd have Roger with you," she said, looking up from her clicking needles. "There are fresh-baked cookies in the kitchen."

"Roger had practice." Why tell her I was mad at him?

"Of course," she said. "I forgot the soccer season has begun. You really ought to have girlfriends, Amy. I know there's Sukie, but she always seems to be sick. I hoped you'd get together with Kimberly Todd. I met her mother at a church social one time. She was very pleasant and said Kimberly was exceedingly shy. Maybe you'd be good for her. Or how about the Shotmeyer twins? They seem like nice girls."

"I don't think the twins want anybody else, Doff. They have each other." I certainly didn't want any talk about my need for friends, and I was on my feet, up the steps and through the front door like something was after me. "Don't worry about it," I called over my shoulder. "I've got plenty to keep me busy. I'm going to do a book report on my new mystery, and I've only read half of it. After I change clothes, I think I'll read."

We've got this wonderful old apple tree out by the back fence, and up in the sprawling branches there are the neatest places to curl up with a book. That's where I headed.

I couldn't concentrate, though. All this stuff was bouncing around in my mind. It wasn't so much Doff I was thinking about. Maybe it was because I was so sure her mother could come live with us. Instead, it was Violetta I was trying to figure out. What would it be like to move to another town? Change schools? Make new friends? And why had they picked Newton Grove? They didn't seem to know anyone here. Sukie said—no, Sukie's father said Mrs. Mills was looking for a missing husband. If she was, what made her think she'd find him here? Was that what she'd come to see the Judge about? Or maybe Sukie got the whole story wrong. It wouldn't be the first time.

I wished I hadn't turned my mind to Sukie. Thinking about her must have brought me bad luck. There she was coming down our driveway heading toward the apple tree.

"Mother drove me over to see you," she called from the corner of the house. "She said I wasn't up to walking so far. She's going to visit with Doff while I talk to you."

"So talk." What was I supposed to say?

"Mother doesn't think I should be mad at you, Amy."

"Mad at me? What have you got to be mad about?"

"Because you're siding with that girl."

"Who said I was siding with anybody?"

"You know what I mean. I don't think you're being very honest either. You were the one told me how crazy she was and now you get chummy with her."

"That's dumb," I said. Somebody must have told Sukie that Violetta and I walked out of the school grounds together. "This is so silly. I'm not chummy with anybody, but if I wanted to be I wouldn't have to ask you."

"But we're friends."

"Look, Sukie, I'll talk to anybody I want to, and if that keeps us from being friends, that's all right with me."

I thought she was going to cry and I hate that, but just then her mother poked her head out the side door of the house and said it was time to go. Boy, that was a short visit.

"You girls can play together another time," she said. "Come along now, Sukie. I have another stop to make."

Sukie lifted her chin and threw one last thought at me. "Just the same, there's something strange about those people. Do they expect to find the missing husband here? Is this where they lost him? Just why did they come to Newton Grove? As long as you're so chummy with that weird Violetta person, why don't you ask her? Ask her about her missing father."

I didn't bother to answer. I would have to admit I was wondering about the same thing. Anyhow, Sukie's mother was already waiting in the car. "Come on, Sukie," she called out, "we're wasting time."

I don't think she noticed that Sukie and I weren't exactly parting with joy. It didn't matter to me.

I went back to my book, but it was too late to get much reading done. Doff called me in to set the table before I'd finished a single page.

"Coming," I called back, and then I remembered what I was going to bring up and I hurried into the house. I was anxious to get it all straightened out.

I didn't wait until after dinner the way we usually do with important matters. As soon as we all sat down and passed the food around I blurted it right out.

"We don't have to worry about finding someone to take your place, Doff," I said. "Your mother can come here."

Doff looked at the Judge and sighed. "Your grandfather graciously suggested that, Luv, but it wouldn't work. Even if Mum could make the trip, which would be very difficult, she wouldn't leave her beloved Devon. All her roots are there. I couldn't ask her to do it."

Grandpa just nodded and smiled. "It was nice of you to think of it, Amy. And I'm glad you're now open to discussion on this thing. Doff and I have been inquiring around, looking at people who might—not take her place—no one could do that—but at least give us an acceptable substitute."

I wanted to turn off my ears, but I'd walked right into this.

"Mrs. Jenkins would come," he went on, "if we asked her."

Mrs. Jenkins. I could almost hear that screechy voice of hers. I groaned but didn't say anything. I guess the look on my face said it for me.

"I know, I know," he said. "Poor Phoebe Jenkins. Not an ideal choice. We'll keep looking."

And there we were right back where we started.

VII

HOW COULD I possibly keep Doff from leaving? Nobody was going to help me, that was sure. I even thought about getting a terrible disease like Roger said, but I didn't know how.

There was another call from England on Wednesday. I was the one who answered the phone. It wasn't mentioned afterward, though. I guess Doff and the Judge both knew how I felt and decided it was better not to bring up the subject unless they had to. That's the way it was at home.

At school things were going better. My fight with Sukie didn't seem to make any difference. During class she kept turning around to borrow my eraser or my pen just like always. And out in the yard, there she was right beside me telling me how sick she'd been and how much homework she had to catch up with. I guess I'm the only one who will listen to Sukie's talking all the time. One good thing, though, she didn't once mention Violetta.

And Violetta—well, she didn't even close her eyes in class again. She still wore that white dress, but nobody seemed to pay any attention anymore.

Once Sukie said, "You'd think that girl would wear something else for a change."

But I snapped right back at her. "Why? If that's what she likes, it's her business." I couldn't help thinking, though, that her mother must wash and iron it every night. All those ruffles.

Violetta kept pretty much to herself too, but when Miss Pritchett dismissed us at the end of the day, I sort of drifted out behind her. We wound up walking those few blocks together until we went different ways. It was my idea, but she didn't seem to mind. At least she didn't tell me to get lost. I had to admit I was beginning to think she wasn't so bad. Maybe I was getting used to her. Maybe I was lining her up with Jessie. Another thing, it turned out she was smart—read better than anybody in class, and in math she was even quicker with the answers than Barney. By Thursday she was just accepted as the new girl.

I was still a little mad at Roger. We walked to school together, but I didn't see much of him after that. There was always practice, and even at lunchtime the boys took their brown bags down to the playing field and booted the ball around when they finished eating.

Then it was Friday—no soccer practice—and as we headed out of the schoolyard at three o'clock there was Roger. Of course, he had his ball with him, and he kept kicking it along as we walked. Sometimes it got away from him and he'd make a big deal of running after it. Dumb. He wasn't acting like Roger at all.

I asked him who they were playing on Saturday, and instead of just saying Calverson, which is about sixty miles north of us, he danced around like crazy and shouted, "We'll cream those Calverson guys—just cream 'em."

When we came to the turnoff, I said, "I'm not going home, Roger. I'm going to see Jessie." Actually, I decided that on the spot. I had enough of the goalie.

"Well," he said, "it just so happens I was thinking I'd drop in at Jessie's myself."

Just so happens. What a show-off.

About that time Matt and Barney came running up behind us.

"Come on, Rodg," said Matt. "Let's have a game. We'll get Danny and Joe and some of the others and go over to Saxon's field."

"Nah." Roger shook his head. "I'm going downtown."

Barney winked at Matt like they had some big secret. "Okay, Rodg," he said, "we know what's going on."

"Knock it off, you guys. I'm just hungry. Maybe later. Maybe I'll look you up later." He kicked his ball halfway down the block and chased after it like a complete goon.

Matt and Barney didn't leave. They just trotted along beside us and every once in awhile they'd whisper to each other and snicker.

Finally, Violetta sort of straightened her shoulders and said, "For the sake of the world, Roger, play with your friends. Or if you really want something to eat, go get it. Amy's coming home with me anyhow, and I don't want any boys around."

I think my mouth fell open. That was the longest speech I ever heard Violetta make. Besides, she said I was going home with her. News to me.

Roger got this funny look on his face. I'd never seen that look before except maybe once when coach bawled him out at a practice game in front of the whole school. And even that wasn't quite the same. I almost felt sorry for him. It would have been all right with me if he came with us, but I kept quiet and pretty soon he just dropped back with his friends and the three of them went off in the other direction.

I wanted to say something to Violetta about going to her place, but I honestly didn't know what to say. We were almost to Main Street by then anyhow.

When we got to Jessie's there was the lady herself standing by the coffee shop door puffing away on a cigarette. As soon as she saw us she rubbed it out in the little ashtray she carries around with her and held up her hand in protest.

"Don't say it, kid. Tomorrow I quit. Tomorrow for sure."

"You've been saying that for years, Jessie. You're a real phony."

"All right, all right. One of these days I'll surprise you. Anyhow, you aren't here from the health department. Come on, I'll fix you something to eat." She nodded to Violetta. "You too, honey."

Violetta shook her head. "Not for me, thanks." And she used her school voice. "I've got things to do."

"I understand." Jessie patted Violetta on the arm. "Catch you another time."

I was kind of disappointed. I thought we'd both eat and then go to the apartment together. I hung back and finally said, "I guess I'm not really hungry either, Jessie. I'm going with . . ."

"No." Violetta, who was already halfway up the stairs, turned and cut me right off. "That's all right. You go ahead. You wanted to talk to Jessie anyhow."

Well, I sure don't have to be kicked in the head. She never wanted me to go with her at all. No reason she should, I guess. I didn't argue about it, just followed Jessie into the coffee shop and headed for my favorite place by the window. In a few minutes I had a plate of fries in front of me and Jessie just across the table.

"Where've you been, kid?" she said. "I haven't seen you for awhile."

"Just around."

"I figured you had things on your mind. Doff leaving and all."

"Who told you about that? Roger, I bet. He's been blabbing it all over town."

"It isn't any secret, kid. She got the message about her mother last Sunday. This is Newton Grove. Word gets around."

That was true, and Jessie wouldn't need Roger to tell her how miserable I was. She'd know.

"Anyhow," she went on, "it wasn't Roger. It was the Judge. He stopped in yesterday. Said it was going to be hard to fill Doff's shoes. Has he found anyone yet?"

"No," I said, "and I'm trying to find some way to make her stay."

Jessie reached over and covered my hand with hers just like Doff did Sunday night. "I know how you feel," she said.

"Doff's taken care of you since you were a little tyke, but if she has to go to her mother there's nothing you can do about it."

They were all ganging up on me—Doff, the Judge, Roger, and now Jessie—using the same words.

"I'm not giving up," I said. "I'm not."

"Don't worry too much about it, kid. Things will be different for you if Doff leaves—and you heard me, I said *if*—but you'll do all right. You're growing up, you know. Does the Judge have anyone in mind?"

"I don't think so. There's Mrs. Jenkins, but we all agreed against her."

Jessie laughed and said, "Heaven forbid!"

Then I had a bright idea. "Jessie," I said. "If there isn't any hope of keeping Doff, how about you? I know you live here at the back of the restaurant, but why couldn't you move in with us? You and I get along just great."

She tightened her fingers over mine and closed her eyes like she was really thinking about it.

I closed my eyes, too, and tried to picture those T-shirts of hers hanging in a row in Doff's closet. To tell the truth, as much as I like Jessie, that was hard. Anyhow, we both opened our eyes again and she pulled a Kleenex out of her apron pocket and blew her nose.

"That's the sweetest compliment you'll ever give me," she said, "but you know it's impossible. I couldn't handle two jobs, and what would I do with this place? It wouldn't run by itself. Who'd feed the townfolk when the mama wants a night out of the kitchen?"

"Ben would be here."

"True, but there are other things. I wouldn't know how to cook for only three people, and I sure wouldn't ever know how to take care of more than one—me. I'm a handful. Besides, you'd have a big problem, kid. I'm going to give up these weeds in my own sweet time." She patted the cigarette pack which was on the table in front of her. "But you'd feel morally obligated to reform me."

Everything she said made sense, and no matter what the Judge thought about Jessie's character, I wasn't sure he'd go for cigarette smoke and orange hair—not in his own house.

"I suppose you're right," I said, "but if I can't keep Doff, I'd rather have you than anyone else."

"I still say it will work out. At least one good thing came out of this past week. You found a friend in Violetta Mills."

"We're not friends," I said.

"Oh?" She looked surprised. "Then maybe you should be. She's a fine girl."

"I don't think the fine girl wants a friend. She sure doesn't know how to treat one."

"Why do you say that?"

"I was supposed to go to her place, Jessie. She said so— told Roger—and you just heard how she wiggled out of it."

"Hmm. I didn't read it that way." She leaned toward me. "I don't think you should either. Maybe she thought you really did want to talk to me. Or maybe she had some other reason."

"You always stick up for people, Jessie, find excuses."

"I just try to give folks the benefit of the doubt. Believe me, Violetta Mills wants a friend. Needs one. I thought for sure you were elected."

41

"If I was, she'd have let me go upstairs with her, wouldn't she?"

"That really troubles you, doesn't it, and you've got a point. Maybe you're right. But you know what I think? I think she's afraid, afraid that if she takes you on as a friend, she'll wind up losing you. And to lose a friend is worse than not having one." She gave my hand another squeeze and stood up. "I'd better get back to work. Tell Doff I hope all goes well with her mother. And look, kid, why don't you give the girl another chance? You could use a new friend yourself, you know."

"I'm doing okay," I said, then thanked her for the fries and gathered up my books. That was when I saw Mrs. Mills come out of the kitchen with a tray of glasses. She was working for Jessie. I didn't know. Maybe that's why Violetta didn't want to come in with me to eat. Still, I didn't understand about being afraid to have a friend. It was hard to imagine Violetta afraid of anything.

As I left, I looked up at the apartment window. There was no sign of anyone around and I ran all the way home.

VIII

THE REST OF Friday afternoon I tried to keep Violetta out of my mind. Couldn't. Sukie said there was something strange about her. Roger thought she was pretty and now Jessie told me she was a fine girl. It was easier back when I thought she was weird. Besides, I seemed to see her everywhere. When I opened my mystery book there she was sprawled across the pages in all her ruffles and at dinner those blue velvet eyes stared up at me from my plate.

Jessie puzzled me too. She always got along with everybody, but she acted like Violetta was special. Another thing, I remembered what the Judge said about having Jessie on your side. Well, if she thought these people were so great, why didn't she suggest that Mrs. Mills take Doff's place? Violetta would come too, of course, and we'd be lumped together whether I liked it or not. Wow! That was something to think about.

All through dinner I didn't say anything but "please" and "thank you." Doff even asked if I was feeling well. I told her I was fine, but in my head I wasn't, and I was still all mixed up at bedtime.

The next day was Saturday. I almost always go to the library on Saturday, but this time I left early—nine-thirty. I wanted to get out of the house. Nothing more had been said about England, but in case there was another phone call I didn't want to know about it. The Judge and Doff were in the yard talking to some man about painting the fence. I just waved good-bye. They knew where I was going.

Sometimes it's still hot in September, and I was in shorts and had on the T-shirt Roger's mother brought me from the lake. It won't be long, though, until the leaves turn red and gold and mornings will be frosty. I think October is my favorite month. I love Halloween.

The library doesn't open until ten, and since I needed a new folder for my book report and had a little extra time, I decided to swing past Steuben's Drugstore. Ordinarily, I wouldn't go down Main Street to get to the library. It's out of the way, but that's where Steuben's is, just beyond Jessie's.

We've got these crab-apple trees planted along the Main Street sidewalk, and I always check them out. The fruit would be ready to pick soon. I wondered what they'd do with it. Doff said last year it just went to waste.

I was thinking about all this as I walked and it seemed no time at all before I was at the coffee shop. I looked in, didn't see Mrs. Mills, but Jessie was at the register talking to one of the bus drivers. I just tapped on the window and when she looked my way I waved.

The stairs to the apartment are right alongside the building and next to the alley. Imagine my surprise when I saw Violetta at the landing and on her way down. She had on jeans and a yellow shirt with the sleeves pushed up. I didn't want her to think I came this way hoping to run into her. I just held up my books and said, "Library."

"It just so happens," she said, copying Roger's voice like you wouldn't believe, "I was thinking I'd drop in at the library myself." Boy, she'd make a terrific actress. I wondered if she was going to laugh but she didn't, and all at once she looked very cross and said, "You don't need to stare. I'm not always in ruffles. I told you I wear what I like. Today I like jeans."

"I wasn't staring," I said. "Or if I was I didn't mean to."

"It's all right." She shrugged and came on down the steps to join me.

She didn't say anything more about her clothes and we just walked along together as though it was the most natural thing in the world, as if we really had planned it.

Newton Grove's a busy place on Saturdays. The farmers bring in their garden stuff and set up a street market in the vacant lot next to the Ford Agency. It starts at eight o'clock and goes on all day.

We do have a huge Food Palace out at the new mall north of town, but most people wait for Saturday to buy their fresh fruits and vegetables. I heard the Judge tell Doff it's a way of saying they don't like the big chains gobbling up everything.

I was thinking about that as Violetta and I went past the empty building that used to be McConnell's Grocery. I guess he was gobbled up.

When we got to the drugstore, Mr. Steuben was out in front sweeping off the walk. He saw us coming.

"Hello there, Amy," he said. "I see you have a new buddy."

Why does everybody do that? You walk down the street with almost a total stranger and people take it for granted you're best friends. I wanted to explain that we hardly knew each other, but I didn't have to say anything. Violetta did.

"I'm Violetta Mills," she said. "New in town."

"Mills. Of course." Mr. Steuben leaned on his broom and squinted at her. "I heard you and your mother came in on the bus last Monday. Staying at Jessie's. Right?"

"Right."

"Well, welcome to Newton Grove. I hope you'll be happy here."

"It's a nice town," she answered politely, and there was that voice again, the one she used for grown-ups. Just the same, I could tell she'd said all she wanted to. I told Mr. Steuben I needed a folder and he followed me into the store to get it.

I took my time, checked to see if the camera I have my eye on was still in the case and stopped to look at the new cassette recorders that just came in. When I went back outside, there was Violetta. She'd waited for me, and she had a question in her eyes. She didn't ask it, though, and the two of us went on without saying a word. Boy, we'd been spending a lot of time like that, a couple of dummies.

I wondered if Violetta would speak up at the library too, and tell them who she was. That was all right with me. When we got there and walked up to the main desk, though, it was Miss Nordoff who took over.

"I thought you'd be back in today, Violetta. I found what you were looking for on Madame Curie." She dug this big book out from under the counter. Then she turned to me. "I see you girls are already friends. I'm not surprised, Amy. Violetta is the same kind of reader you are. There's no satisfying her appetite for knowledge. She's been in every day since she got to town.

Violetta said, "This is a good library."

I managed a smile and we headed for the books. Violetta apparently found what she wanted in the biography section, and I found a book about cats. Someday I'm going to get a kitten. We sat at one of the big tables and read awhile. Then we checked out what we wanted and left together. We didn't have to do that, I know, but it didn't hurt anything.

We were half a block down the street when I noticed Violetta had that look again, that questioning look. Finally, she said, "Why did you do that? And twice."

"Do what?" I didn't know what she was talking about.

"You let them call us friends. We're not friends."

My very words to Jessie, but somehow out of Violetta's mouth it sounded as though she was sorry we weren't. *Give her another chance.* I spoke right up. "I wish you wouldn't say that. "

"You mean I'm all right now because I'm wearing jeans?"

"That hasn't anything to do with it. I still think those ruffles and bows are silly, but I'm getting used to them. If it's what you want, whoop-de-do for you." Then I told her about my wearing gym shoes last year on Easter. "Even Roger was against me on that. Said they looked stupid. But Doff went along. She called them 'inappropriate,' but if I wanted to look odd that was my business. 'Self expression' or something like that. Anyhow, I was comfortable."

"Well, whoop-de-do for you," said Violetta.

After that it went a little easier. The truth was there were some things I liked about Violetta. Maybe I was wishing we were friends. I decided the time had come to get one thing straight.

"Okay," I said, "there's something I need to ask. Why did you tell Roger I was coming home with you yesterday? Truth now."

Violetta didn't hesitate. The blue eyes were clear and honest. "I wanted to get rid of him."

"Then you weren't really inviting me?"

"Not really," she said, "but not for the reason you think. Why should you want to come to my place? It's just a room."

For a minute I wasn't sure what she meant. It's funny how you take living with lots of space for granted. Remember when I thought I'd simply die up there with no place to put my things, and I thought Violetta didn't mind? Where did I ever get that idea? Sure, she moved a lot, changed schools, lived all pinched together in one room over Jessie's kitchen. That didn't mean she liked it. She did what she had to do. I could see that now, but how do you tell someone you think she's brave without sounding slushy? If I could be Doff for a minute or the Judge or even Jessie, maybe I'd know the right thing to say.

We'd come to the Oak Street corner—one way to town, the other to my house—and we'd stopped walking. I had to say something, and all I could do was tell her the way I felt.

"It's not just a room," I said, "when the person who lives there is someone you like."

The smoky blue eyes misted over and Violetta turned away from me. I decided I'd said something she didn't want to hear, and I waited for a sharp answer. I was sorry, but I was also wrong. When she turned back to me, her eyes were clear again and she was smiling.

"Did you really want to come upstairs with me yesterday?"

"Of course. I thought you asked me, and I didn't say no."

"Then if you still want to come, what are we waiting for?" She tossed the hair out of her eyes, and this you won't believe—she put her arm right through mine and we marched off like that to Main Street.

IX

THE APARTMENT over Jessie's kitchen was pretty much as I remembered it except for the unmade bed. It was the couch, of course, pulled open and taking up most of the room. The sheets and covers were scrambled together and heaped in the middle.

"Mother must have slept late," said Violetta as she scooped up the bedclothes and tossed them in the corner. "She worked last night."

When she started to fold the bed back up again, I didn't know whether to help or not, so I just stood there like a stick. Then, while she put the cushions in place and punched them down so they fit right, I took a long look around the room. There sure weren't any stuffed animals. In fact, even most of the small things I saw belonged to Jessie—the digital clock, ashtrays, trinket boxes. Not that it surprised me. How much can you carry with you on a bus? I didn't see suitcases either, but I remembered that there was a small closet just inside the door. That's where Doff would put suitcases.

There was one thing that was new, though—a framed picture on the chest of drawers against the side wall—a picture of a very blond man with dark-rimmed glasses. He had on a plaid jacket and held a pipe in one hand. It looked like a snapshot that had been enlarged.

Violetta, who was now finished with the couch, must have been watching and noticed where my eyes settled.

"That's my father," she said. And I knew by the way she looked at me that the subject was closed.

Wow! Sukie's bossy voice rang through my brain. *Ask her about her missing father.* I sure wanted to. Doff says it's all right to be "direct," but she also says you shouldn't touch sore spots. Violetta's look said this was a real sore spot. I'd have to wait until she told me about him herself. I wondered if she ever would.

It took only seconds for me to think all this, but Violetta wasn't watching me anymore. She'd gone into the bathroom with the stuff she'd tossed in the corner. It was almost as if she'd forgotten I was there. But when she came back, she spread out her arms in a kind of welcome and said, "All right, this is it. The Upstairs Hilton. I hope you didn't expect much. We don't even have a TV."

"Look," I said, "I don't care. But if you'd like to watch TV, we can go to my house later. We have all afternoon."

"Maybe you have," she said. "I've got things to do. Don't you have chores?"

"I'm supposed to keep my room straight." I was embarrassed to say that. Doff is always picking up after me. "And sometimes I set the table—things like that."

"I guess it's different when you have someone working for you."

I was the one who told her Doff worked for us, and I should have explained right then how it really was, that she was almost family, but I didn't.

"Anyhow," she said, "my chores can wait awhile. It's time for lunch. Are you hungry? There's peanut butter, plenty of bread and milk, and I bought apples yesterday."

"That's fine. I grew up on peanut butter."

Violetta seemed to be a different person in her own territory. We made the sandwiches together and she poured milk into two Bambi mugs she took from the shelf above the sink. I remember when Jessie got those on her trip to Disney World.

While we ate, we actually talked to each other. I told her about the kids in school, how the twins always stuck together, how a lot of the girls chased after boys all the time, how I wasn't into boys except for Roger, and I explained about Roger. I also told her about my reading tree and that she'd have to see it sometime.

Violetta didn't tell me quite as much, but I did learn that she wasn't into boys either and that she'd been in five different schools since first grade. How about that?

By the time we got down to the apples, she cleared things away and said she'd better get busy. "I'm taking the laundry downstairs. Jessie lets us use her machines. You can come with me if you want, or," and she gave me a long blue velvet look, "you can go home to your reading tree. I wouldn't blame you. It sounds great."

"I'll come with you," I said. "I was invited here, wasn't I?"

I helped carry the box of clothes and the detergent down to Jessie's laundry room, which is at the back of the restaurant, separate from her living space. It has an outside entrance, but Violetta had the key. She loaded the machine with sheets, towels, socks, underwear and, yes, there was the white dress.

"I use cold water and don't let it run very long," she said. "That way I can dump everything in together."

She flipped the switch and said we had half an hour or so. What should we do?

I told her about the street market and that we could go there and look around.

She said she'd like to see it. Jessie had gone out real early to get stuff for the restaurant.

Like I said, the lot is next to the Ford Agency almost at the end of Main Street and we headed for it. Market day brings everybody to town, and along the way several people stopped us to say hello and ask about the Judge and Doff. Most of the fifth and sixth graders had taken the bus to Calverson for the game, but we saw some of the older kids. Matt's brother, Rick, zoomed past us on his in-line skates. Then suddenly he turned and came back. He's in junior high and hardly ever looks at me. As a matter of fact, he wasn't looking at me now. It was Violetta.

"Hi, Ryker," he said. "Thought you'd be over in Calverson rootin' for Roger."

"I didn't sign up for the bus," I said. "There's more in my life than soccer."

He didn't care anymore about my answer than he did about his question. His eyes were still on Violetta as he took off again. He kept looking over his shoulder and I thought sure he was going to crash into one of the apple trees.

"Boys," said Violetta. "And I wouldn't like to be called by my last name."

"I don't mind. Roger started it."

"You said Roger was your best friend. I would have thought your best friend would be a girl."

"Who?" I asked. "Sure, there's Sukie. We used to get along pretty good, but you can see how that's going."

We had wandered onto the market lot, and we picked our way around the tables of squash and tomatoes and sweet corn—everything the farmers raised. It was early for pumpkins, but there were a few small ones. I told Violetta about the Pumpkin Faire that we have in Newton Grove the end of October. It's usually combined with Market Day and all the Main Street stores put up Halloween decorations and have sales.

"At school," I said, "we have open house as part of the celebration, but best of all we have this contest for the most original pumpkin heads. Even though you don't have to enter you can get extra credit and it's fun."

"It sounds like fun," she said. "I hope I'll still be here."

"What do you mean you hope you'll be here? Jessie said you move a lot, but you just came."

She didn't answer that. Instead she said, "What else did Jessie tell you about us—my mother and me?"

"She said some nice things. She likes you." I avoided the bit about needing a friend.

"Jessie's good to us. We get the apartment and all the meals we want. Besides mother keeps her tips. I even get paid to do odd jobs. It's a great deal."

"If I had a meal deal like that I'd stuff myself all the time with those fries. I'd be a blimp."

It didn't take long to use up our half hour and more. I bought a sack of popcorn, big enough for the two of us, and we worked our way back to the laundry.

Violetta transferred the wash to the dryer. The white dress though, she set aside and hung on a hanger she had brought down from the apartment.

"Can't let this shrink," she said, "or come to pieces. Nobody in class would recognize me if I didn't have my ruffles." She kind of laughed and I joined in.

"We can go back upstairs if you want," she said. "There's no use waiting here. It takes forever for the towels."

I agreed and followed her. When we got to the top of the steps, the apartment door flew open and Mrs. Mills rushed out to meet us.

"I wondered where you were, Letta," she said, all excited. "I was on my break and wondered where you were."

"Doing the wash, Mother. I've just been doing the wash." She touched my shoulder. "This is Amy."

Mrs. Mills didn't even look at me. "Oh, the wash. Everything's all right then," she said. "But did you get my uniform? Did it get in?"

"Sure. It was hanging in the bathroom. I found it."

"Oh." She sounded relieved. "I'm so glad. I meant to put it in the hamper, but I forgot." She laughed and said, "I'll remember next time. Honestly I will."

"It's all right, Mother. I found it." Violetta took hold of her mother's arm and we all moved into the apartment. Again Violetta introduced me. "This is Amy, Mother, Amy Ryker, the girl I told you about."

So she told her about me. I tucked that away in my mind as I said, "Hello."

Mrs. Mills gave me a quick glance. "Amy?" she said, and it was like a question. Then she turned back to Violetta. "I'm just on my break, Letta—have only a few minutes, but sit down and let me tell you about this man who came into the coffee shop this morning. He's from Middleton." She leaned close to Violetta and whispered, "He said he'd come back tonight. I think he knows your father."

Something about Mrs. Mills bothered me. I didn't know what it was, but I was sure she didn't want me here. I felt like I'd been caught listening at the door—hearing secret stuff. My stomach felt kind of mushy and I wanted to get out of there. I had told Violetta I had all afternoon, but now I said, "I'm sorry, I have to go." I didn't give any excuse.

Violetta looked over her mother's head and said, "You don't have to leave." But those smoky eyes were saying something else, something I couldn't understand.

My mouth was suddenly dry, but I managed to say, "It's okay, I'll see you later." Then I eased out the door and closed it quickly behind me.

X

I WAS SO GLAD to be out of that apartment. I wanted to talk to somebody. Oh, not Doff or the Judge or even Jessie. It had to be someone my own age. Last week I'd have gone straight to Roger. Not now. It was more than being mad at him. I just wasn't ready to share with him what I knew about Violetta. I'd just have to think it out by myself. I turned off Main Street and then took my time going home. There was no hurry.

Think it out. That's what I needed to do. Was I bothered because Mrs. Mills ignored me? She did that the day she came to see the Judge. And I couldn't be upset because maybe someone had found Violetta's father. He wasn't anything to me. No. It was something about Violetta and her mother. There I was stuck. What was it?

When I came dragging in our back door at four o'clock, I still had no answers. Doff was emptying the dishwasher and she looked up to say I was early. She hadn't expected me until dinnertime. "Is anything the matter, Luv? Are you feeling all right?"

She asked me that yesterday too. I must look as bad as I felt, but this time, too, I said everything was okay.

After dinner that night, Roger called. Since I wasn't at the game, he wanted me to know they won. We didn't talk long. I told him I was busy. There was no call from Sukie, which was just as well. Sukie can get you to tell about stuff when you don't really want to.

On Sunday, Grandpa said he wanted me to drive over to Grundy with him to see a Mrs. Honeycut. Someone down at the courthouse told him she might take care of us when Doff left.

"I know you don't have any heart for the mission," he said, "but you ought have a say in the matter."

We didn't talk about it anymore than that. I'd already decided I wouldn't like her. Besides, I had something else on my mind and as soon as we got out on the highway, I said, "Tell me about my mother." Maybe there was a clue there someplace that would help me with this "thinking it out" business.

Grandpa didn't seem surprised to have me ask, but he waited a minute before he said, "I'm sure you know what there is to tell, Amy." And then he repeated the story I already knew by heart.

My mother had no family, came to Newton Grove with foster parents in her senior year of high school, married my father right after graduation, had me, and . . .

He stretched it out, of course, and I could see his hands tighten on the wheel as he talked. Oh boy, he was going to tell me about the accident again and I didn't want him to. No matter how big and strong and important the Judge is he always chokes up when he even thinks about the accident. I wished I hadn't started this, and I interrupted.

"What I really want to know, Grandpa, is what my mother was like."

"Well, let me see." He seemed to let down a little and I thought he was going to be all right. "She was a sweet little thing," he said. "Windblown hair, brown, lighter than yours. But you have the snapshots. You know. She loved Doug— your father. Said she'd follow him anywhere." Then I heard the catch in his voice. "And she did."

Grandpa held his eyes straight ahead of him on the road and squeezed the wheel even harder than before. I felt so sorry for him. I still hadn't heard what I wanted, but there'd be no good trying to ask anything more now. Grandpa just wasn't with me.

You see this whole thing about my parents is real sad. Grandpa explained everything to me before I started to school. Just in case kids asked. I was only five, but I remember listening. I even cried, but it wasn't because of the story. It was because Grandpa cried. The accident didn't mean much to me. It happened to strangers. I didn't know my parents. My family was Doff and Grandpa and I was happy. I took the box of snapshots they gave me—there were only a few—and put them away in the bottom drawer of my dresser, way at the back. That was that.

It wasn't until Sukie moved to town that it was all pulled out again. She was the one with the questions. Had to know everything. Why did I live with my grandpa? Where were my parents? What happened to them? This was when we were in the fourth grade and already she was going to be a newsperson. She was especially interested in the accident. My mother and father on a motorcycle, no helmets, crashing into the concrete rail around Devil's Curve.

"Wow!" she said. "A page one story." But even Sukie got tired of it and went on to dig up other stories and put mine back where it belonged. Mostly it was forgotten.

Generally, people who do remember don't bring up the subject, not around Grandpa anyway. But once in awhile it pops up by itself. Last year when Doff and I went to the centennial parade some lady I'd never seen before stopped us in the street and peered at me through thick metal-rimmed glasses.

"You're the Ryker child, aren't you," she said. "Judge Ryker's poor little granddaughter. Such a sad thing."

I found out later she'd taught in the high school way back, retired to Florida, and was just here on a visit. Anyhow, I was glad we didn't have Grandpa along.

Another time I found him standing in front of our fireplace shaking his head at the picture of my father. He was mumbling to himself and he didn't know I heard him. "Just a kid," he was saying, "a teenage kid. What a waste."

Grandpa hates motorcycles.

Grundy's in the next county and we still had a way to go. There was a church service coming on the radio and I flipped the dial. We'd already been to church. We don't get too many stations, but I found some music. It helped to pass the time.

After awhile Grandpa came back to himself and he reached over and patted my knee. His voice was steady again when he said, "Now that Doff is leaving, it's only natural for you to think about your mother. She wasn't in the family very long. I didn't get to know her as well as I would have liked, but I'll always tell you whatever I can about her."

Maybe he couldn't tell me what I really wanted to know. Would my mother go to Jessie's with me for a hamburger and would she hold me by the hand?

I asked no more questions. We were pulling into Grundy, and "the mission," as Grandpa called it, was to see Mrs. Honeycut. Like I said, I'd already made up my mind about her, but I hadn't counted on Grandpa's high hopes.

"This lady might be just the ticket," he said. "I understand she has a lot of spirit, is in good health, loves young people and has motherly qualities. What that last means I'm not sure, but let's go into it with an open mind. Agreed, Amy?"

He'd been in such a dark mood I wanted to cheer him up, and I said, "Agreed, Grandpa, an open mind." The least I could do was give it a whack.

He had written the address in his little black notebook, and we found it with no trouble. The house was white with green shutters, and there was a picket fence that gleamed with new paint.

Grandpa nodded in approval. "So far, so good. Everything kept in fine shape. Mrs. Honeycut takes care of things."

The door, painted green to match the shutters, looked almost too big for the house, and in front of it was a white mat with green lettering—"WELCOME AND WIPE YOUR FEET."

"She's also clean," said Grandpa.

I wanted to laugh, but I wasn't sure this was funny. I wiped my feet before we rang the bell.

The door opened right away and we were swept into the

room by the largest lady I'd ever seen. I don't mean fat, I mean big. The Judge is tall. He told me once he never quite made it to six feet, but he's up there, and this Mrs. Honeycut towered above him. And she had shoulders like a linebacker.

"You must be the Judge," she said. "It is a pleasure to meet you." She sort of bent down to take hold of his hand and shook it until I'm sure I heard the bones crack.

"Well, yes," said Grandpa, rescuing his fingers. "I thought perhaps we could talk. I understand you might be available . . ." His voice trailed off. Mrs. Honeycut wasn't listening. She had turned to me and stooped to a crouch. She took my face between her two giant hands and squeezed. I thought my eyes would pop.

"And this," she said, "is the little darling I'm to care for."

I gave Grandpa a look that was a real cry for help. I knew he'd save me.

"Mrs. Honeycut," he said, using his courtroom manner, "it's going to be awhile yet before Amy needs caring for. This is just an introductory visit. I'd like to have you send me a letter with your background and qualifications and the terms you would expect." Grandpa's quick.

She was disappointed I could tell, but she pulled herself up to her full height and backed off. "I understand," she said.

Grandpa took her hand—carefully I noticed. "Be assured," he said, "we will remember you."

That was the closest to a lie I ever heard from the Judge. But it really wasn't a lie was it? And as we left, I said I'd remember her too.

Safely away from the white house, everything seemed pretty good. Grandpa said, "I'm hungry, Amy. How about a pizza?"

That was a silly question to ask me, and we found a place that looked busy. Grandpa said that's the way to pick a good restaurant.

"Can I get everything on it?" I asked as soon as we were seated.

"Everything. And I'll join you."

"Wow! I didn't even know you liked pizza."

"There are a lot of things you don't know about your grandfather. We should go out together more often. You're getting to be quite a young lady."

How about that? Everybody is telling me I'm growing up. First Doff, then Jessie, and now the Judge. Well, maybe I am. After all, I'm almost twelve.

XI

EVEN THOUGH I'd been busy with the Judge all day Sunday, I hadn't forgotten that awful feeling I had up there in Violetta's apartment and that there was something I had to think out.

A new school week was starting, and I wondered whether Violetta would say anything about Saturday, about her mother. Maybe there was nothing to say. Maybe that's just the way Mrs. Mills was and Violetta was used to it. But what about her father? Was he really found? Would Violetta tell me? Sure, she knew now that I liked her. She'd linked her arm in mine and we'd had a great day, but that didn't mean we'd share every secret thing. I remembered how she clammed up when I saw her father's picture.

Anyhow, on Monday Violetta acted as though nothing had happened over the weekend. She also wore regular clothes like the rest of us. Then Tuesday and Wednesday went by and it was the same. I still walked to school with Roger. You can't break a habit that's been going on since kindergarten. But he wasn't ever around after school, and Violetta and I drifted out together just like we'd been doing. It wasn't quite the same though. I was careful what I said. I didn't want to sound nosy. Besides, Violetta seemed to do most of the talking. She still didn't mention Saturday, but she rattled on about unimportant things, how she thought Miss Pritchett should wear green more often because it matched her eyes and how the Shotmeyer twins looked so much alike she couldn't tell them apart—stuff like that.

She didn't ask me to go home with her again, and when Saturday came I didn't get to the library. The crab apples were ready and I found out who was getting the fruit. Anybody who wanted to pick it. Doff said if I'd bring home enough for a few jars of jelly she'd put them up for us. She also said I could help. A weekend project.

That's the way it went, one day just sliding into the next. Violetta didn't wear the white dress again. It was too summery, I guess. We began to eat lunch together, and Sukie hung around the edges, not wanting to be friendly to Violetta but sugaring up to me. Sukie hadn't been absent again either. I think she was afraid she'd miss something.

The boys were slaves to Coach Tompkins, but they still cornered Violetta in the halls or at recess—wherever they could. She was pretty good at dodging them, but sometimes I came to her rescue. Roger insisted he wasn't interested. She was just a girl. He only hung around to watch Barney and Matt make idiots of themselves.

That's a laugh. I have eyes.

Another Saturday went by without the library. I promised Roger I wouldn't miss the biggest game of the season, and it was an all morning ride to Fairfield. I asked Violetta if she wanted to go, but she said no. Soccer wasn't for her.

All this time she was getting better and better to be with, and she was talking so much—not too much, I don't mean that—she was just letting go. The subjects she brought up began to change too, more about herself. She said she really liked math, getting the numbers to come out the way they were supposed to, and, you know, she didn't think she was pretty at all? She actually hated that white-blonde hair of hers.

One day when I was complaining that Mr. Anderberry was too strict with his monitor system and his crossing guard patrol and his rules about no loitering in the yard, she told me about a school she went to in third grade. It was a city school and in a rough part of town.

"I was afraid all the time," she said. "But I didn't want to tell my mother. A lot of the big boys carried knives and liked to scare the little kids. I used to walk out of the grounds beside this big eighth-grade girl—pretended I was with her. She didn't ever know that. Then when I got to the corner I'd start running for home. I was always sure one of those guys was behind me. For once I was glad to move."

That's what I mean about talking a lot. Sometimes Violetta's words just came rolling out like a recording, and she went from one subject to another without taking a breath. She couldn't stand fried egg sandwiches, thought yellow the next best color to pink, and hated being tall, always in the back row. One thing she liked about herself, though, was her name, Violetta. And when she said it, it really did sound like music.

Finally, and it was bound to happen, she got around to me. We were into October by then, and some of the trees were already showing color. One afternoon we were poking along Oak Street wishing the red and gold leaves could stay on the trees all winter. They were so pretty. All of a sudden she surprised me by saying, "I heard your Doff's leaving. I'm sorry."

"Thanks," I said, "but where have you been. It's no secret. Everybody in town's known about Doff for a long time."

"Well, I didn't. But that's not the point. The point is when Jessie told me I said there shouldn't be any problem—plenty of live-in help around."

I started to say something, but she stopped me.

"No, listen. When Jessie explained about Doff, I was *really* sorry, but how was I to know? Then she told me about your parents too."

"That's no secret either. Did she tell you what happened to them?"

"No, only that they were dead. I guess she figured you'd tell me yourself someday."

I wasn't ready to tell her right then and I let it drop.

The next day I invited Violetta to come to my house.

"I told you about my reading tree. I think you should see it."

"It's about time," she said, with fake sarcasm. "I was beginning to think you'd made the whole thing up." It was nice to be joking together like that and we laughed.

It was Friday. We didn't have any homework, and I figured we'd have a couple of hours before dinner. Then, as we left the schoolyard she said, "You won't mind if we go by the coffee shop will you? I'd better tell Mother where I'll be."

"You can call her from my house."

"No. I'd rather see her. She might want me to do an errand or something. Besides, I can change clothes."

It was wasting our time, but if she'd be happier about it, it was all right with me and I said so.

I wasn't excited about seeing Mrs. Mills again that's sure, not after the last time, but I'd stay out of the way.

It worked out all right. Violetta's mother was busy with a customer and Jessie said she'd give her the message about going to my house. "Your mother's working through the dinner hour tonight," she said. "You don't have to hurry back. Have fun. I'm glad to see you two together." She winked at me.

Violetta dashed upstairs, put on old jeans and then she looked in to see whether her mother was still busy.

"I ought to wait," she said, "and talk to her when she has a minute."

"Jessie'll take care of it," I insisted. "She won't forget. Jessie never forgets anything."

She gave in but seemed a little nervous as we left.

At my house Doff greeted us with the same happy look Jessie had. I could tell she was glad I'd brought a girl with me.

I decided I might as well change clothes too, and upstairs in my room Violetta just stood in the middle of the floor and gasped. I saw her eyes go from the bright red comforter on my bed, to the bookcase, to the desk, to the posters on the wall.

"This is really something," she said.

"If you think this is something, you ought to see Sukie's room. She even has her own TV with cable."

"I'd settle for this. I've never had a room of my own."

I didn't tell her I'd never had to share one. "Find a book if you want," I said. "There aren't many biographies, but I do have a good one on Belva Lockwood. It was a present from my grandfather. I think he wants me to be a lawyer."

I put on some old clothes and we went back to the kitchen. Doff said, "You don't need to tell me where you're going," and handed each of us a brown bag. "Just a few nibbles and some grape juice to keep you happy while you read."

"Thank you very much," said Violetta politely, and in a few minutes we were settled in the cupped branches of my tree.

"I like your Doff," said Violetta. "I bet you hate her leaving, but where in the world did she get that name?"

"From me. Actually her name is Dorothy, but I couldn't say that when I started to talk. Everybody calls her Doff, even the Judge."

"Were you with your mother before Doff came?"

"Not just before, and I can't remember back to her. I was awful little. I do remember when Doff first came, though. The Judge thinks I've heard the stories so often I've claimed them as my own memories, but that's not so. One thing proves it. Nobody knows what's in your dreams but you. Right? Well, soon after Doff came, when I was still sleeping in a crib, I used to dream I was falling, not scary or anything, just sort of drifting down, turning over and over like a spacewalker. Someone always caught me, someone warm and soft who held me in her arms and sang to me. Doff was the lady all right. I told her about it a long time after, and she sang the same song to me, a lullaby she said she learned as a child."

69

"She sounds almost the same as a mother."

"Almost isn't enough. If she was really my mother, she wouldn't leave me."

"I suppose that's true. I know my mother won't ever leave me."

Our talking just sort of stopped there. It was as though Miss Pritchett had raised a hand for quiet and announced that it was reading time. Both of us opened our books.

How many people are there you can sit and read with without saying a word? Not Sukie, that's sure. And Roger wasn't a reader. We always used the tree for climbing when I was with him. And now here I was with this new girl, our backs against the trunk of this wonderful tree, bent over our books and knowing we'd talk again when we were ready—only when we were ready. How comfortable it was. And less than a month ago if you'd told me this would happen I'd have said you were crazy out of your mind.

I don't know how much later it was—I took off my watch when I changed clothes—when Doff called from the back door.

"Violetta. Your mother's here. She wouldn't come in. I told her where you were."

Almost at the same minute, Mrs. Mills came hurrying down the driveway from the front of the house. She had on her white uniform and her hair was pulled back and tied with a ribbon. Wisps of it had come loose and straggled over her cheeks and neck. She was breathless as though she had been running.

Violetta jumped down from her perch and ran to meet her.

"Are you all right?" she said.

"Oh, Letta, I wanted you to come downstairs and eat with me on my dinner break and you weren't there."

"But, Mother, you knew where I was. Jessie said you were working through. I thought you might wait to eat until you'd finished. I'd have been home by then."

Mrs. Mills's eyes filled with tears. Tears. I couldn't believe it.

"Oh, I knew where you'd gone," she said, "but you hadn't come back."

Violetta put her arm around her mother's shoulders. "I'm sorry. I'll come back with you now."

I was still in the tree pretending not to listen, and Violetta called up to me. "Thanks for everything, Amy. I'll see you at the library tomorrow." And she walked with her mother down the driveway.

The other time these two had left our house together they'd been hand in hand, and remember I decided it was a mother thing and kind of nice. But this was different. I had the same mushy feeling in my stomach that I'd had up there in the apartment, and I said, "Sure, I'll see you tomorrow."

It was only after they were gone that I climbed out of the tree and gathered up the brown bags and the books and went into the house.

Doff hadn't come out while Mrs. Mills was there, and when I joined her in the kitchen she said, "I didn't want to intrude. I hope there's nothing wrong."

"No, there isn't anything wrong," I said. "Violetta just had to go home."

XII

DOFF DIDN'T believe me when I said there was nothing wrong. I knew she didn't. No questions, though. She lets me alone. If I want her help, she knows I'll say so.

This was part of that other thing I needed to think out, Mrs. Mills acting so strange up there in the apartment. Today she hung onto Violetta like she was afraid she'd get away. Do mothers do that? Mrs. Adams shouts a lot, but she always handles things, and Mrs. Enslow never gets excited. One time she found Roger's pet garden snake curled up in her rocker and she just picked it up and tossed it out on the patio. But I had this creepy feeling that if Violetta wasn't right there to grab onto, Mrs. Mills would be totally lost.

Well, I still wasn't going to think any of it out now. It had been three weeks since Grandpa and I had our mission with Mrs. Honeycut, and there had been no more interviews. Nothing more had been said about England either and no more phone calls—at least none that I was told about.

Mrs. Enslow said she was sorry Doff had to leave. She had a brunch for her—invited all the neighbors. The church ladies gave her a party too, but Doff didn't say much about any of it.

I was beginning to think the whole problem might just disappear. The months would go by, and the years, and I'd grow up and go off to college and Doff would still be here.

That was the way I was looking at things on Saturday morning, and I was glad Violetta said she'd meet me. At first I thought she might change her mind, but I decided she'd not only come, she'd probably say nothing about what happened, just like the last time after I'd gone to the apartment.

When I got to the library she was there all right, sitting on the steps waiting for me, but I was wrong about the other part. Right away she said, "Go ahead, ask me about my mother."

She sounded almost mad, and I remembered how she'd been that first day when I found her on my front porch.

"What do you mean?" I asked.

"Don't play dumb. You know what I'm talking about."

"Okay," I said with a little bite in my own voice, "but why should I ask questions? It's none of my business. Come on, let's go inside."

She didn't move, just sat there looking straight ahead. I was thinking how close I'd felt to her yesterday in the apple tree. I wondered what she was thinking.

Then all at once she leaned forward and put her head in her hands. If this had been anybody but Violetta Mills I'd have told you she was crying.

"It was all my fault yesterday," she said. "I should have checked with her before I went to your house. I knew I should." She didn't sound mad now, just unhappy. "Sometimes my mother gets—well—kind of upset—if I'm not home when she wants me."

I wasn't ready to hear about this. I put my books on the steps and sat down beside her.

"I know how that is," I said, trying to make it seem like I had the same problem. "I'm always supposed to report to Doff where I'm going and when I'll be home." Mostly that was true, but I wasn't fooling Violetta.

She let her hands drop to her lap and looked at me through the strand of pale hair hanging over her eye. "You know it isn't the same," she said, "but I'm sorry. I've never told things like this to anybody before. I shouldn't talk about my mother."

"Sometimes I think you have to talk. Besides, you didn't tell just anybody. You told me, and I guess when people are friends this is the kind of thing you tell each other."

When I said that, Violetta pushed the hair back off her forehead—and this sounds awful weird—there was a kind of brightness on her face.

"You mean we're friends, Amy?" she said. "Really friends?"

"Sure." I was a little embarrassed. "Why not?"

I've never had anybody look at me the way Violetta did then—right into my eyes. It was like she was hunting for something—proof maybe. I blinked but I didn't turn away. I couldn't.

When she spoke again her voice was low and soft. "I've never had a friend before."

"Well, you've got one now." I intended to be flip. I was all choked up and I didn't want to end up blubbering.

Honestly, I don't know what I'd have done if it hadn't been for Matt's whistle. It came sharp and clear from way down Pine Street, and for once I was glad to hear it. Let me tell you Matt's whistle is something. He doesn't use his fingers. He just tucks his lips together in his own special way and blows. It really hurts your ears. After the second blast I squinted off down the street to see the boys zooming toward us on their skateboards.

"Here they come," I said to Violetta, "the triple threat."

Matt and Barney were in the lead with Roger trailing behind. Roger's not as good on the boards as they are. His mother hates the things and pressures him. I think Mrs. Enslow would rather see him behind the wheel of her van than on that skateboard.

Actually, Roger was doing better today as he came to a stop in front of the library and I told him so. I also said, "How come you guys are in town? I thought there was a game over in Dawson."

"Canceled," said Roger. "Half their team's sick."

"They heard how good we are," said Barney. "Chickened out."

"We thought we'd go fool around downtown," said Matt. "Want to come along?"

"Not I," said Violetta, right off. "Busy."

"Have you got money for treats?" I asked.

Matt did a quick turn around Violetta. "Maybe. Won't that change your mind . . . Vi? Is that what they call you? Vi?"

"No," she said, "it doesn't change my mind, and my name is Violetta."

"We could buzz out to the mall." Barney again. "See what's happening. Split a pizza maybe."

I knew he meant both of us. Barney and I get along fine, but I wasn't the one he was looking at.

"Way out there?" I said. "You're crazy. Besides, we're working on ideas for our pumpkin heads." That was what I had in mind for today. I just hadn't had a chance to tell Violetta.

All this time Matt and Barney were making fancy moves around us—over the curb and back again. Doing all the tricks they could think of. They were trying to show off for Violetta, of course, and Roger, poor Roger, was kind of in the background like an outfielder.

Violetta got to her feet. "Show's over," she said and headed for the library door.

But Roger wasn't going to be left out. "Hey, you guys," he yelled, "watch this," and he rocketed off down Pine Street beyond the library. It's downhill in that direction and that part of Pine still has potholes left from last winter. Even so, he might have been all right if he hadn't turned around to wave at us. His timing was off. I could see what was going to happen, but there wasn't a thing I could do about it. Halfway down the next block he banged against a parked car, his skateboard flew out from under him and he landed in a heap alongside the curb.

"Holy Christopher!" shouted Matt as he wheeled down the street with the rest of us close behind.

The heap sat up. At least Roger wasn't dead. He was a mess

though. His T-shirt was torn and dirty. His arms were scraped and kind of bloody.

"Are you okay, Rodg?" asked Barney.

"Did you break anything?" said Matt. "I mean besides the taillight on Jim Tobbin's VW?"

Roger ran his tongue around his mouth and said, "I guess my teeth are all okay. If I broke those two front babies, my dad'd kill me."

"And you can do that for yourself," said Violetta who had moved up beside him.

It was then that Roger started to get up, but when he leaned on his right arm for support his face went white. I'm not too good with pain and I wanted to duck out and let the rest of them take care of this, but how could I? It was Roger sitting there all battered and probably with a broken arm.

"I can call your mom from the library," I said, "if you want me to."

He shook his head. "Nah, I better do it. She'd think I was dead for sure if she got a message from somebody else."

"Doc Willoughby's office is just down around the corner," said Barney. "I could go get him."

"If he's just around the corner," said Violetta, "and if your legs are all right, Roger, we can go to his office. You can call your mother from there. Why don't you two," and she nodded at Matt and Barney, "help him up. Just don't jar his arm."

Violetta was definitely taking charge, and it seemed the most natural thing in the world. While she was talking, the boys pulled Roger to his feet, a little clumsy but not bad. I guess they remembered the first aid talks we had in class.

It was funny there weren't any other people on the street. It all happened so fast and with very little noise. No one had even come out of the library. Besides, this was Saturday. Most folks were down at the Main Street market.

Violetta waited until Roger steadied himself and then she said, "Will you be all right?"

"I'm okay," said Roger.

"If you hold your arm close to you and keep your other hand under your elbow," she said, "I don't think it will hurt too much."

"Hey, Violetta," said Matt, and I noticed he said her name real slow. "How come you know so much?"

"Experience," she said. "When I broke my arm I remembered what they told me to do. That's all."

Just the same she was the star. We must have looked a little crazy as we paraded around to Doc's. Matt and Barney, carrying the skateboards, walked on either side of Roger in case he needed a shoulder to grab, and Violetta stayed close behind them to be sure all went well. Nobody paid any attention to me.

The arm was broken all right. Doc took one look and ordered X rays. Roger called his mother and in ten minutes Mrs. Enslow drove up in the van and took over. We hung around though until Roger came out of the back room with a cast from his fingers to his elbow and a sling to hold the weight.

"Skateboards," said Mrs. Enslow. "I hope you'll listen to me now and get rid of the thing before you break your neck. And you've even been begging for in-line skates!"

"Gee, Mom, the only trouble is I'm just not good enough yet. What I need is more practice."

"Even you can see that's out for awhile. Come on, we'd better get home."

"Boy," said Barney, "there goes the soccer team."

He would have to throw in a little extra gloom, but Mrs. Enslow said, "Let's not worry about that now. Tell you what. Why don't you all come up to the house for lunch. I have lasagna in the oven. Your goalie will need some cheering up."

"Yeah," said Roger, "come on, you guys."

See what I mean about Mrs. Enslow never getting excited?

The lunch idea was fine with Matt and Barney. They never turn down food, but Violetta thanked Roger's mother and said she couldn't. As for me, I wanted to go, but I begged off too. I don't think Roger cared whether I came or not. Like I said this was happening a lot lately.

The boys piled into the van and after it pulled away Violetta said, "I'll walk back to the library with you to return my books, but then I have to go home. It's almost twelve-thirty. That took the whole morning."

"You make a good nurse," I said, as we ambled back around the corner.

"I've thought of it."

"I hope I never break a bone. How did you stand being in a cast? It's awful, isn't it?"

"I wouldn't know, Amy."

"What do you mean?"

"I never broke my arm. It was my mother, but I did learn a lot. That part was true."

XIII

AT FIRST IT puzzled me that Violetta said she was the one who broke her arm. What did it matter? But then, I figured it out. She didn't want the kids to know how much she helped her mother. I wasn't going to make a big deal out of it, and as we poked our way back to the library I got us onto another subject.

"I was hoping," I said, "that we could start looking up some characters for our pumpkin heads. You got any ideas?"

"There's plenty of time yet." She didn't sound too excited. "Besides, we're not supposed to tell anybody what we choose, are we? Keep it a surprise?"

"That's not a real rule. And it's more fun to work together. I'm thinking of doing Mary Poppins with her umbrella. Or maybe Pinocchio."

"Shouldn't it be something scary? After all, it is Halloween."

"Oh, there'll be plenty of witches and gobs of ghosts, but

it's the clever ones that win. Last year the twins did Tweedle Dum and Tweedle Dee. Twins for twins. They got first place for fifth grade."

"Doesn't anybody just hollow out the pumpkin and make a regular jack-o'-lantern?"

"Sure, but anybody can do that, and you have to wait until almost the last day. Otherwise your pumpkin rots before the judging. I always get an extra one, though, to carve. Got to do that. It's part of Halloween."

"I know," said Violetta. "We always have a jack-o'-lantern. No matter where we are. Then we go trick or treating—Mother and I."

"Your mother doesn't have to take you around in Newton Grove. It's safe here. Doff hasn't gone out with me for years. I just go with Roger."

She kind of laughed. "I didn't mean Mother took me. We go together. She always has a good costume too. Last year she was the Wicked Witch of the West. You know, from Oz. I think she had more fun than I did."

I was always learning something new about Mrs. Mills; it wasn't hard to picture her having a good time at trick or treat. It was when I tried to imagine Doff with a black hat and a broomstick that I ran into trouble. Thank goodness there was no need to mention it. We were back at the library.

Violetta turned in her books and took only a few minutes to pick out a couple of new ones.

"Sorry I can't stay with you," she said. "Mother's off this afternoon, and I promised I'd go shopping with her. We may even walk out to the mall."

After she left, I felt kind of lost. To tell the truth I didn't want to stay at the library myself now. Mary Poppins could wait. Violetta was right. No hurry. Besides, maybe this afternoon was the thinking-out time I'd been needing. The question was where to go. Actually, the library ought to be all right. If I went off in a corner, nobody would bother me. But I just can't concentrate with all those books around screaming to be read.

My apple tree wouldn't do either. It's within shouting distance of Doff and the Judge and anyone else who happens by.

As I checked off one place after the other, I just started to walk, not paying any attention to where I was going. Don't ask me why I headed off toward the edge of town. I just needed to be moving.

I guess I moved fast, because before long I ran out of sidewalks and almost out of houses. Then I saw where I'd wound up. I was standing right in front of the entrance to the cemetery—where my parents are buried—and Grandma Ryker too. I'd been here lots of times. Grandpa brings me. This was the first I'd ever come by myself, though, and even if I hadn't planned it, I decided I might as well look for the graves. Grandpa'd probably be glad if I did, and anyhow, hadn't I found the perfect thinking place? There's nothing quieter than a graveyard, and I seemed to be the only person around.

They call it Woodlawn Memorial Park, and even though the grounds are closed in by a high iron fence, the gate was open in a kind of welcome, and it is a little like a park inside—pretty. The grass is always cut and watered and so green in the spring and summer. There are a lot of big trees along the fence and others scattered on the hillside—sumac, oak, maple. The leaves were mostly red and orange now and some had already fallen. They rustled under my feet as I walked.

I remembered that the graves were close together, and I was sure I could find them. We always followed the main path up the slope to the first—no, the second turn. Then off to the right, counting one, two, three giant steps and we were there. And I was there now, standing in front of a gray stone marker which was laid even with the ground. I stooped down and brushed away the dead grasses that had collected on the letters.

MARY ELIZABETH RYKER

WIFE AND MOTHER

There was a space beside it for a second stone—Grandpa's. Thank goodness he wasn't ready for it, not for a long, long time.

You might think it wasn't right that I stopped at Grandma's grave first and not my parents, but it was the way Grandpa did, that's all. Actually, the other marker was just beyond the first and it was bigger, covering two spaces.

RYKER

DOUGLAS/MARIAN

I like the name Marian. I wish they'd given it to me. Of course, that isn't what I would have called her. What would I have said? Not "Mum." That was Doff's English word. Not "Mother" either. It sounds so stiff, straight up and down, even when Violetta uses it. "Mom?" I don't think so. Roger calls Mrs. Enslow "Mom." Okay for Roger, but not for me. "Mama?" That was it. Back in fourth grade, Miss Rasmussen read us a story about a twelve-year-old pioneer girl who called her mother "Mama." It seemed just right, and it always led to their talking together.

It was weird to be here thinking about my mother. I'd never done it before. I'd been around a lot of mothers and never thought about mine. Maybe, like Grandpa said, it was because Doff told us she was leaving. Or maybe after meeting Mrs. Mills, I wondered what kind of a mother I would have had. She'd have mended my clothes, I guess, and baked birthday cakes. Doff does those things. But would she have taken me to the movies and been a witch on Halloween? Most of all, would we have talked together?

I sat down cross-legged on the ground in front of the double marker and touched the letters of her name. "Mama," I whispered, liking the sound. "Mama, what troubles me about Mrs. Mills?" I blurted it right out as though I expected an answer. I didn't, of course. I'm not that dumb. It's just that I wanted something.

I closed my eyes and tried to imagine my mama sitting here on the grass beside me, maybe putting her arms around me. But all I could see in my mind was a snapshot of a girl with windblown hair and a big smile. And she was a stranger. All three of the people buried here were strangers. It was funny. I could get a feeling of Grandma Ryker, but she was the only one. I guess it was because there was a place for her in my world right beside the Judge. But Douglas and Marian didn't fit in at all. They belonged just to each other. Wherever they are, I hope they're happy.

I opened my eyes and looked again at the marker, rubbing my hand across the smooth part of the marble and tracing the grooves of the letters with my fingers. *Marian.* She never really got to be a mother. She wasn't with me long enough.

I patted the stone in a kind of good-bye, got up and brushed off my jeans. I hadn't paid any attention to the time, and now when I looked at my watch I was surprised that it was almost four. How could it be so late? Not that it mattered as long as I got home in time to help a little with dinner.

I wasn't sorry I'd come, and it had been good to ask my question out loud like that. I thought of Mrs. Mills again and how Violetta sort of took care of her. Somehow, it seemed like Mrs. Mills never got to be a mother either. *There, I'd answered my own question. Violetta didn't have a real mother anymore than I did. That's what troubled me.* I turned away from the graves and with just one quick look over my shoulder, I hurried along the path to the gate and then home.

XIV

NOW THAT I knew what troubled me, what would I do? Talk to Violetta? Maybe. She'd already shared a lot about herself with me. It shouldn't be too hard. I'd talk to her first chance. I thought about it all the way home, but when I finally turned up our front walk I found something else to deal with. Roger was sitting at the top of the porch steps with his back against one of the posts and cradling that dumb cast with his good arm. He didn't look very happy, and I felt sorry for him.

"It's about time you showed up," he shouted at me. "Where you been?"

I canceled my sympathy. "Nothing that would interest you," I said, "or your friends. Have they gone home?"

"Hours ago. And we've been calling all over for you. You weren't at the library. I thought you were with Violetta, but Jessie said she was off with her mother. I even checked Sukie.

Boy, she's such a noodle. Wanted to know everything. I thought I'd never get off the phone."

He seemed to be awful upset, and I said, "Is there something wrong?"

"Only that Doff had another phone call. She has to leave for England as soon as possible."

I swallowed the lump in my throat. I'd made myself believe this was all going to blow over and she wouldn't really go, but her plans had never changed. She just kept still about them.

"So," I said, trying to cover my hurt, "what did they want me for? To break out in tears?"

"I'm trying to tell you. Doff had some business to tend to in the city and wanted to stay for a few days with a friend, someone she knew in England. The Judge drove her over. They left about two. He wanted you to go with them, but they couldn't find you. It's a pretty long drive, at least five hours, I guess, and he's going to stay overnight and come back in the morning."

"Oh, rats," I said. "And what am I supposed to do while he's gone?"

Just then a demanding voice came from deep inside the house.

"Is that Amy out there with you, Roger? Is she finally home?"

It was a loud, screechy voice that had to belong to Mrs. Jenkins.

"Okay, Roger," I thrust my thumb toward the house, "what's she doing here?"

"Don't get mad at me. None of this is my fault. Here." He held out a folded piece of notepaper. "The Judge asked me to wait around for you and give you this, but if you're going to yell at me, I ought to just tear it up and go home."

I grabbed the paper and read Grandpa's bold black handwriting.

I wish you had been available to come with me, Amy. It would have been pleasant to have your company on the return trip. But so be it.
Please bite your tongue and give Mrs. Jenkins full cooperation. I'll be back tomorrow.

I barely finished the note when Mrs. Jenkins appeared at the front door. Maybe I haven't mentioned this, but Mrs. Jenkins is skinny as a post and always wears her hair in tight curls that look like they're still in the rollers. I don't think I've ever seen her smile.

"You might have answered me," she said, as she stood there wiping her hands on Doff's best apron. "At least you're home. I'm staying with you tonight. The Judge has gone to the city with . . ."

"I know," I interrupted. I didn't need to hear it all again. "Roger told me."

"Fortunately," she went on, "I was able to be of service. I would have preferred more notice, though. It's not easy to work in someone else's kitchen."

She made it sound as though she'd been dragged here by her curls, but I answered politely, "I'll be glad to help." After all, Grandpa asked me to cooperate.

"Good," she said, looking at me over the top of her glasses. "When you have time, I'll be in the kitchen."

She backed out of the doorway and disappeared as I called

after her, a little louder than I should have. "I'll be in in a few minutes. As soon as I talk to Roger."

"Don't bother," he said. "Not if you're going to yell again."

"I'm sorry. I shouldn't have been so cranky. I guess it just hit me that I really am losing Doff, and I haven't been able to do anything about it. Maybe I was blaming you for not finding a way for me to keep her here. When your life is going down the drain, you've got to blame somebody."

"Well, it doesn't have to be me. I got troubles of my own. Why don't you blame Violetta?"

"Don't be silly."

"Or did you tell her you didn't expect any help from her because she was weird?"

"I don't think that anymore. Violetta's all right, and Jessie told me she needed a friend."

"That's a switch. She sure isn't exactly the most friendly person in the world herself. I've decided she really is weird."

"How can you say that after the way she helped you this morning? She was super and you loved the attention. You know it."

"She just felt sorry for me—thought I was dumb. Probably went home and laughed herself silly over my broken bones."

"You can't fool me, Roger Enslow. You like her and you want her to like you. Only you might as well forget it. She told me so. Of course, that was a stupid thing you did. I feel terrible about your arm, but face it, you never were much good on that skateboard."

"Knock it off. Talk about a ruined life. I'm out for the soccer season and nobody cares."

"You've got Matt and Barney."

"That's what you think. They went home right after they ate. Bored. They're over at the school grounds right now messing around."

My sympathy came back. It was a little like the old days with Roger and me. "Come on," I said, "I'd better go in, but you don't have to leave."

We trailed into the house and headed for the kitchen where we found Mrs. Jenkins on the step stool searching the cupboards.

"Things are so awkwardly arranged here," she complained as she climbed down. "And there's a drip under the sink that I wouldn't tolerate for a minute." She opened the little doors to show us.

Roger pushed past me and peered into the opening. "You're right, Mrs. Jenkins, you've got a real drip here. Come on out, Sukie Adams. Come out of there. We've found your hiding place."

I couldn't help but giggle. Roger's such a nut. But Mrs. Jenkins didn't get it.

"What are you babbling about?" she said. "What kind of nonsense?"

"It's just a joke," I said. "Not a very good one, but a joke." I gave Roger a dirty look. He didn't need to make things worse than they were.

"Well, I don't see anything funny." She frowned at me over her glasses. "What I need now is a large cooking pot or I'll never be able to fix dinner."

"There's one right here in the lower cupboard," I said, stooping to get it out for her. "What are we having?" I wasn't hungry. I was just trying to smooth things over.

"A specialty of mine," she said. "Cabbage rolls and boiled potatoes—good stick-to-your-ribs food."

Yuck. "Can Roger stay for dinner?" I said, shooting him a desperate look. It would help to have a friend around.

"Well," Mrs. Jenkins hesitated, "I'm not sure there's enough for three."

"I'd be glad to share," I said quickly. But Roger didn't wait for the answer to that.

"Hold it," he shouted. "I can't stay anyhow. Dad's barbecuing hamburgers and I promised Mom I'd finish off the lasagna we had for lunch." And he headed for the back door.

I followed him outside, but I couldn't think of anything mean enough to say, so I just watched him hurry across the yard to the alley. The traitor. Time was when he'd have eaten grasshoppers if I asked him to. We were that close.

When I went back inside, Mrs. Jenkins was scrubbing out the pot I'd found for her.

"You can get a towel and dry this," she said. "And by the way, where were you this afternoon when they were looking for you? It isn't my place to say, but I would think you should tell the Judge where you go. Maybe he doesn't mind, but wouldn't your Grandma Ryker be upset with you if she were here?"

I noticed she'd left Doff out of it altogether. Anyhow, I told her where I'd been. "And Grandma Ryker wasn't upset at all," I said. It was another dumb joke, and Mrs. Jenkins didn't even smile. She backed off a little, though, and admitted it was nice of me to visit the graves.

There weren't any more questions, but nothing stopped the talking—about Violetta—Mrs. Mills—Jessie—and everybody else she could fit it. Then she brought the conversation back to the leaky sink.

"It's not my place to say, but I'd sure have someone out to fix that double quick if I was taking over here. Not saying I am, you understand. Not saying that at all."

I hoped not, because even the thought gave me shivers.

Mrs. Jenkins talked through dinner—and I did eat half a cabbage roll—choked it down with milk. Then she talked through the cleanup and would have talked right on until bedtime if it hadn't been for the phone call. I jumped on the first ring and dashed into the den to answer it.

XV

I THOUGHT IT might be Roger ready to apologize, but it was Sukie who answered my "Hello."

"I'm sure you'd rather talk to that girl," she said, "and you haven't been very nice to me lately. I'll bet you don't even remember the important date that comes up this week."

I was glad she couldn't see my face. I really had forgotten, but it took me only a minute to get my head together.

"Your birthday!" I said. "How could you possibly think I'd forget that?" Notice it wasn't a lie. It was a question.

"Okay," she said, "I guess you did remember. Anyhow, you always help me hand out the invitations to my party, and I've got them all ready, all twenty-six of them."

"You're inviting the whole class again—after what happened?" I was really surprised. For two years Mrs. Adams insisted on having everybody in Sukie's class at her parties. It was one thing she and Sukie agreed on. For Mrs. Adams it meant the democratic way. Miss Pritchett's been teaching us about that. And for Sukie it meant a lot of presents. But last year was such a disaster, I didn't think they'd go for it anymore.

There was a great sigh on the other end of the line.

"It's a long story," she said. And I settled down in Grandpa's big leather chair. I might as well be comfortable while she talked. As Grandpa would say, I was going from the frying pan into the fire. Now instead of listening to Mrs. Jenkins, I'd be listening to Sukie.

"My mother did say no at first," she began. "Last year was so bad. That klunk of a George running wild through the house, knocking over her crystal lamp. And your Roger not much better. He and Matt wrestling around in the living room. Then all the spilled food, the water fights and the . . ."

"I remember," I interrupted. "I was there."

"Anyhow, right off Mother said I should invite just six girls, my best friends. We would have a small party, lunch maybe and a movie. 'It will be dignified,' she said."

Sukie has to dramatize everything, and I admit she was pretty good at mimicking her mother's whiney voice.

"Well, I told Mother that wouldn't do. I'd have a terrible time deciding who to invite."

Sukie started naming off the girls in the class, and I let the phone hang limp in my hand. The reason it wouldn't do, of course, was that there would be only six presents. Besides, I wasn't sure there were six girls in the class who would come. Sukie isn't all that popular. She was still rattling on about how she couldn't possibly limit her party to six when I lifted the phone back to my ear and said, "So that's when you went back to the whole class?"

"No, not yet. Mother said, 'Then let's just have the girls. How many are there?' I told her fourteen and she said that would be all right. We could play the usual games, pin the tail on the donkey, drop the peanuts in the bottle, and we'd have cake and ice cream. It would all be neat and orderly."

"If your mother liked that idea what made her give it up?"

"I'm coming to that. I told Mother that wouldn't do either. The girls in sixth grade don't want to play baby games, and they probably wouldn't even come if boys weren't invited.

"My mother threw up her hands at that, and then my father got into the act. 'If you want to be democratic, Edna,' he said, 'you have to be nonsexist. Besides, a crowd's a crowd. You might as well have a big one.' And that was it. My mother flip-flopped right back to inviting the whole class. But there was a condition. She said, 'All right, Randall, we'll invite everybody, but it's your responsibility. I won't have any more destruction. You'll have to plan something to keep those horrible boys in hand.' "

Just then I heard Mrs. Jenkins clattering around in the living room. I think she wanted to know who was on the phone, or maybe she just wanted to send me to bed. I don't know. I was getting tired of all this anyhow.

"Okay," I said, "what did your father come up with?"

I was sorry I asked because she was off again.

"That's another whole story," she groaned. "My father thought we ought to have a tour of the *Sentinel*, you know, see how the paper's put together, the new computers and all that. 'It would be on a Saturday,' he said. 'You could even have lunch in the employees' cafeteria.'

"Well, you can bet I voted that down. Going through the newspaper would be boring and too much like one of Miss Pritchett's field trips. We might as well be in school."

All at once there was dead silence on the line. I waited. I knew there had to be more, and I waited.

At last in an impatient squeal she said, "Well, aren't you interested in the rest? Why don't you ask me what we decided?" I could almost hear her grinning.

"Okay, Sukie, what did you decide?"

"Just listen to this. My father is taking over the Family Fun Center out at the mall for the entire afternoon. We'll have the whole place—the video games, skit ball, the food, everything. All to ourselves. And free. Isn't that super?"

"Super," I said. It sounded like a wild afternoon and free for everybody but Mr. Adams.

"There'll be twenty-six kids," said Sukie. "That's more than last year." Then her voice dropped to an uncertain whisper. "Do you suppose they'll all come?"

"Don't worry. They'll come." I was sure they would, even the boys. Dangle a deluxe pizza in front of any guy in Newton Grove and he'll do most anything. And here they'd get the entire fun center—free. Wow!

"You'll help me hand out the invitations on Monday then? Please, Amy. I think some kids will come just because you're my friend. You are still my friend, aren't you?"

"Sure, Sukie, I'm your friend, and I'll help. But I have to go now. I have a problem. I'll see you."

When I went back into the living room, Mrs. Jenkins was

sitting straight and stiff in Doff's armchair. I swear she had moved it closer to the den so she could hear my conversation. That was all right. There wasn't anything secret about it. What wasn't all right was what she said.

"Do you always talk that long on the phone?"

"Actually, I wasn't doing much of the talking," I said. "Sukie was."

"And you have no time limit on your calls?"

"No, not really. Doff says I get bored if people keep me on the phone too long."

Mrs. Jenkins shot a look at the clock over the mantel. "And you don't think this was too long?"

"Guess not."

"Well, I would think a time should be set, but of course it's not my place to say."

No, not again. If she throws that at me once more I thought, I'll scream. But it was just a thought. I wouldn't really scream. I bit my tongue like Grandpa said and kept still. Thank goodness he'd be home tomorrow.

XVI

GRANDPA CAME BACK the next day, Sunday, just like he said he would, and he must have gotten up awful early because he made it by noon. Boy, was I glad to see him. I'm sure he knew how I felt about having Mrs. Jenkins there. Almost the first thing he did was drive her home.

People are sure different. Grandpa, who really had a right to know, didn't ask me where I was on Saturday. Of course, I told him. Not everything though. None of the stuff about my mother and Mrs. Mills.

Mostly what we talked about after we got rid of Mrs. Jenkins was Doff. I wanted to know why she had to leave so soon.

"It seems," Grandpa said, "the woman who is with her mother has a family emergency of her own. Anyhow, we knew this was coming. It's no surprise."

"But Doff said she'd be here awhile yet, and I hoped . . . well

. . . that if I just didn't think about her leaving it wouldn't happen. She wouldn't leave at all."

"Problems don't disappear that easily, Amy. We always have to face up to them. And Doff said she thought you were facing this very well."

I wasn't, of course, but I gritted my teeth and kept still.

About two o'clock we decided we were hungry enough for dinner, and we went to Jessie's—fried chicken and chocolate cake. Violetta's mother wasn't working and neither one of them was around. Jessie said they mentioned going on a picnic over at the grove. No matter. I hadn't planned on seeing Violetta until Monday, and I wouldn't have talked to her now anyhow when I was with the Judge.

Jessie came over and sat with us when she had a few minutes, and we told her the latest about Doff. When she found out we didn't have anybody lined up to take her place yet, she said, "I'm sure the right person will come along, but if you need cleaning and laundry done in the meantime, Ben's wife, Ruthie, might be willing to help out a couple of days a week. She's a good worker."

Grandpa said we were all right for now but thanks anyway.

After dinner there was a football game on TV and when I got bored I read one of the books I'd brought home from the library. Then in the evening we had popcorn and apples and played checkers. I won too. And don't think he let me. Not Grandpa.

You know it was one of the nicest Sunday nights I remember. It wasn't until bedtime that I thought about it being one without Doff.

The next morning it was funny to come down to the kitchen

and not find her at the stove. Instead, there was Grandpa poking in the cupboard for cereal. Orange juice and milk were already on the table. He knew where to find those. We decided last night I'd eat lunch in the cafeteria. I don't usually do that.

We left the house together. Grandpa said he was going to walk to town, and I headed for Fletchers' corner where Roger was waiting.

I was glad he was there, and I'd had such a good Sunday I was willing to forgive him for leaving me alone with Mrs. Jenkins.

"You missed a great dinner the other night," I said. "The cabbage rolls and the boiled potatoes were dee-licious." We both laughed and were friends again. I even offered to carry his books for him. He was having trouble hanging onto them with only one good arm.

We weren't early getting to school. Most of the class was already there, including Violetta, but I didn't get to talk to her because the bell rang.

Miss Pritchett knows about Sukie's parties, and because the whole class is always invited, she even gave her a few minutes of class time.

"Sukie Adams has a surprise for you," she said, making it sound very special.

Mrs. Adams always insists on inviting the teacher too, and Sukie gave Miss Pritchett the first envelope. She probably wouldn't come. The other teachers didn't. They have us all week, why would they want us on Saturday too? But Miss Pritchett said, "Thank you," all the same.

Sukie stuck some invitations in my hand, and as I shuffled

through them I noticed I had the one for Violetta. I knew Sukie would like to leave her out, but democracy is democracy.

Practically everybody opened the envelopes right off, and there were a few squeals of joy. Of course, girl birthday parties aren't all that big with the boys, but Matt whistled and George Gunner said, "Cool." A free afternoon at the Fun Center was no small deal.

When the last invitation was delivered, Miss Pritchett put us right to work. The rest of the schoolday was like any other.

Of course, I had that thing about mothers on my mind all day, but since Violetta and I didn't eat lunch together I didn't get to really talk to her until we were on our way home. Roger didn't try to come with us. He was going to hang around school for awhile, go down to the field and watch practice even if he couldn't play.

As we left the schoolyard I wanted to bring up my visit to the cemetery right off, but I decided it would be better to lead up to it. I edged into conversation by telling Violetta how I'd forgotten Sukie's birthday. Then I said, "You're going to the party, aren't you?"

She took the envelope out of her jacket pocket and turned it over a couple of times. I saw it hadn't been opened.

"Is that what this is?" she said. And not waiting for an answer, "No, I won't go. She doesn't want me there."

"What difference does that make? It'll be a good party. Sukie's parents always do neat things. Why should you miss out on the fun? Besides, you'll be there with me."

"All right." She shrugged, "If you want me to, I'll go."

"Good," I said. Then I told her about Doff's being gone and about my night with Mrs. Jenkins.

"That woman sounds horrible," she said. "Sure not like your Doff. I wonder what your grandfather would have said to her. He's used to nice people around him. Jessie told me your grandmother was wonderful."

"I guess she was."

"Jessie also said she liked your parents. 'Great kids' is what she said."

"I don't know much about them." It wasn't my parents I wanted to talk about. It was Violetta's mother, but because it was the right time, I gave her the whole story, wound up even telling her about going to the cemetery on Saturday.

When I'd finished she said, "I'm sorry. I didn't mean to be nosy. You probably don't like to think of all that."

"It's all right. It doesn't bother me. Douglas and Marian were my parents, but they don't mean anything to me."

"At least you know where they are."

"What good is that? You've got your mother alive and with you. You're lucky."

"Yes, I'll always have my mother." I saw her fingers tighten round the books she carried. "She needs me."

We had come to our turn-off and I had to say something to keep her talking. "I know you do a lot around home. I admire that. I don't do much."

"You'd do things if you had to. Right now you and your grandfather are getting along alone, and I bet you help."

"Big deal. Doff had everything washed and cleaned and ready for us. Wait till the clothes pile up and the house gets dirty. Besides, you take charge sometimes. I couldn't do that."

"Sure you could."

I thought for a minute she was going to let the conversation end there. I didn't want that to happen yet, and I was glad she made no move to leave. She stood there holding her books close to her as if they were protecting her, and . . . well . . . she just stood there. Finally, in that quiet voice she uses when she's dead serious, she said, "Look, Amy, there's something I need to tell you. Because I really feel you're my friend now. My mother is a great person and people like her. She can always find work. She supports us. Jessie told me she's the best help she's ever had. But sometimes she's not like a mother. And there's one thing she can't deal with."

I didn't know whether she wanted me to say anything or not, but the questions were already on my tongue. "It's your father, isn't it? It's true that she's looking for him?"

Again there was a long wait. Then she nodded. "That's why we move all the time. She asks people if they know him. She describes him to strangers and asks if they've seen him. Sometimes someone says maybe, and we're packing again."

"How did you happen to come to Newton Grove?" I remembered that was one of Sukie's questions.

"A face in a newspaper picture—outside your own grandfather's courtroom. She follows any clue. Sometimes when there's nothing, she just picks out a place on the map where she thinks he could be. She's so sure that one day she's going to find him and we'll be a family. We'll have a house and a dog and a parakeet and everything will be rosy. But there's never any sign of him. It's stupid."

Violetta's words came out faster as she talked and her voice was shaky. I reached out and put my hand on her arm. "Maybe it isn't stupid."

"No. You don't understand. He may even be dead. But even

if he is alive we won't find him. He doesn't want to be found. Amy, my father left us before I was born."

I let that sink in, but there wasn't anything I could say. It didn't make any difference. This time I knew it was the end of the conversation. And this time it was all right with me.

All at once her face brightened. "Hey," she said. "It's getting late. I'll see you tomorrow."

That was it. I'd had my talk with Violetta. The truth was I'd learned more than I wanted to.

XVII

ON TUESDAY things at school settled back to boring. At least we had Sukie's party to look forward to and, of course, the Pumpkin Faire and Halloween coming up. Violetta and I spent a lot of time together. We didn't talk about mothers and fathers again, but our friendship was stronger. I could feel it.

Grandpa and I were managing pretty well alone. Like I told Violetta, Doff had left us with drawers full of clean clothes and a spotless house, and she'd also made a couple of casseroles and put them in the freezer for us. Some of the neighbors, especially Roger's mother, invited us for dinner or sent food over, and we could eat out if we wanted to. We were doing okay, but I still couldn't imagine being without Doff forever. I tried not to think about it.

Grandpa gave me money to buy a present for Sukie, and when Violetta and I went shopping I found a couple of tapes she wanted. I had decided to do Mary Poppins for the contest, and we discovered the perfect hat at the thrift shop—black with flowers around the brim. I'd have to have a narrow pumpkin—no fat one like I had last year for my Cheshire Cat. Grandpa was contributing his black umbrella and I practiced drawing faces with a marker pen.

I shared all of my ideas with Violetta, but she didn't tell me what she was planning. I wondered if she had something in mind or if she had decided to wait until the last day, and like she said, just carve out a scary face.

By Friday everyone was talking about the party. Sukie was the center of attention and she loved it. We were to be at her place at two, and Mrs. Enslow was going to drop Roger and me off there on the way to some meeting. I wanted to be sure Violetta was still going, and I told her she could come to my house and go with us if she wanted to.

"That's all right," she said. "I'll go on my own. I've got things to do in the morning."

I had things to do Saturday morning too. I was even skipping the library. Doff was coming home the first of the week and Grandpa and I wanted to clean up the kitchen for her. Not that we were messy, but we wanted her to find things just the way she left them.

It was kind of fun working with Grandpa. We scrubbed and polished until everything shone. It didn't take long either, and by the time Mrs. Enslow honked for me I was scrubbed and polished too.

When Roger and I got to Sukie's I looked around for Violetta. She wasn't there. At least not yet. Sukie stood on the front porch and took all the presents handed to her. I noticed

Mrs. Adams put them into a big carton and Sukie told me they'd take them out to the Fun Center and she'd open them before the party was over so everybody could see what she got.

For the ride out to the mall we were going to use the Adams' station wagon, one of the *Sentinel*'s vans, and the Shotmeyers' four-door. Mrs. Shotmeyer had volunteered to drive so we could all be properly buckled up. It was decided she'd take five of the girls and Mrs. Adams the rest. I was to sit up in front with Sukie. Mr. Adams would take the boys. All twelve of them showed up. I knew they would.

I kept watching for Violetta, but she still hadn't come by the time we were ready to leave, and I wondered what could have happened. I asked Sukie if Violetta had called her at the last minute.

"No," she said with a smirk. "But I told Mother I didn't think she'd show. Probably didn't want to buy me a present. So she misses the party. Who cares?"

Not Sukie, that was sure, but I cared. I cared a lot.

We could all have walked to the mall, but it is pretty far and with cars it took only a few minutes.

The Family Fun Center is a great big place with a high ceiling and polished wood floors and bright colored posters—red and purple and green—all around on the walls. And they have everything there you can imagine. Video games, old-fashioned pinball machines, an ancient jukebox with some fifties music. There's even a little roped-off section where you can dance if you want to. And the food! Pizza, hot dogs, muffins, make-your-own sundaes. I can't name everything. There are benches and tables down by the food too, so you don't have to stand

and hold stuff while you eat. The Fun Center's super, all right.

The girls got there first. The doors weren't open for us yet, and we just gathered around Sukie to wait until the van pulled up and Mr. Adams let the boys out. Mr. Adams is a big man and he has a booming voice to match his size.

"If you'll get in two lines," he shouted over the commotion, "I'll give each of you a packet of tokens to use however you wish. You have the place to yourselves, so it won't be crowded. No need to push and shove. The management has supplied their usual attendants. Go to them if you have any problems. Enjoy. And when the party's over we'll see that you all get home."

It was too noisy for anybody to answer him, but a few of us started to clap and everybody joined in. It was a kind of thank you. Mr. Adams left then. I think he was glad to get away.

When the doors opened we knew they were ready for us. There was already the smell of buttered popcorn and sizzling hot dogs and pizza sauce. Some of the boys went right to the food, but there was also a dash for the games. Sukie and I headed for a Nintendo. We have a bet on, and so far I'm ahead.

Actually, things went pretty smooth. Keeping the attendants on duty was the smartest thing Mr. Adams did. When George and Matt started roughing it up while they waited for hot dogs, this one big guy moved in and threatened to send them home. Everybody got the message. Mrs. Adams stayed in the background. I think she would still have liked six girls for lunch. I really missed Violetta, and kept an eye on the door thinking she might still come, but after awhile I gave up.

Nobody used the dance floor. No, I'll take that back. The

twins did, but I wouldn't call it dancing. The boys kept as far away from it as they could.

I hung around with Sukie part of the time, and I helped her mother bring in the presents from the station wagon and stash them on the table by the ice-cream booth. She told me that before everybody used up their game tickets she'd bring in the birthday cake from the bakery next door and they'd sit down to be served. Then Sukie could open the packages. I'm not sure anybody cared to know what she got, but that was the plan anyhow.

Everybody seemed to be having a good time, but after about an hour I found Roger sitting by himself over by the door.

"It's a pretty good party," I said.

"Yeah, it's all right. But I'm not going to wait until it's over. I've had all I want to eat and I can't do much left-handed. I called my mom. She said she'd pick me up after her meeting —about four-thirty or so. I explained to Mrs. Adams."

"Violetta never did come," I said. "I hope nothing's wrong."

"Why should anything be wrong? She and Sukie hate each other."

"But she said she would."

"Probably just changed her mind. Don't worry about it."

But I did worry. They don't have a phone in the apartment or I'd have called her.

It was maybe four when Mrs. Adams had the cake and ice cream ready and asked the attendants to get everybody to the tables. "And be sure to announce," she said, "they can go back to the games after they've eaten."

Finally, when everyone was served, Sukie started ripping open the presents and holding each one up for us to see.

There were a lot of nice things—scarves, a coin purse, books. Most of the boys brought things their mothers bought for them I'm sure. And when Sukie shouted, "Hey, look at this perfume from Davey Hofstead," everybody laughed. Poor Davey, he's so shy. I don't think he even knew what was in his package.

Roger gave her a diary. I know that was Mrs. Enslow's idea.

And then there was the thing from George. No question that he'd taken care of it himself. It was wrapped in newspaper and tied with string, and when Sukie opened it she let out a scream. I was sitting next to her and leaned over to see a snake coiled up ready to strike. It was fake, of course, rubber, but it looked awful real. I would have screamed too, if I'd been the one to open that package.

"George Gunner," Sukie shouted when she got her breath, "I don't think that's funny." To be honest, I don't think George meant it to be funny. He loves those things, has a whole collection.

By the time Sukie got down to the last two or three presents, I slipped away and found Roger again. He was still there by the door.

"I'm going to call Jessie," I said. "I hate to bother her at the restaurant, but I really am worried about Violetta."

There was a pay phone outside the center, and when I dialed the number, I waited the longest time for an answer. Finally, Jessie said, "Hello," and I blurted out my question. Had she seen Violetta?

"Oh, they've gone already." She sounded a little impatient. "Left at noon."

"Gone?" I said. "Where did they . . ."

"Look, kid," she interrupted, "I'm awful busy right now,

up to my armpits in customers and working alone. Why don't you come on down and when I get a break we'll talk."

I said, "Okay," and after I hung up I tore back to Roger. "I'm going home with you," I said. "I'll just tell Sukie good-bye and thank Mrs. Adams. Only be a minute."

"Well, hurry," he called after me. "Mom just drove up."

XVIII

═══

ON THE WAY back into town, Mrs. Enslow said she had an
errand at the drugstore before we'd go home and she hoped I
wasn't in a hurry, that the Judge wasn't waiting for me.

"No," I said. "Besides, I'm going to Jessie's and you'll go
right past there. I have to see her about something." I didn't
say what. I could tell Roger wanted to know about my phone
call, but I didn't feel like talking.

When we got to Main Street he told his mother he was going
along with me.

"That's quite all right," she said, "but my chauffeuring is
over for the day. You can get home on your own, and don't
be too late."

He agreed, of course, and when we got out of the car at
Jessie's, he said, "Okay, Ryker, tell me what's going on."

"I don't know myself," I said, "but I'm going to find out."

We were in luck. Ben had just come in to take over in the kitchen and brought his wife along to wait table. Anyhow, Jessie had time for a short break. She bustled us back to her apartment and got right to the point.

"Violetta and her mother took the noon bus to Middleton," she said. "I'm sorry, kid. I just assumed you knew they were leaving. I asked Violetta if you were coming down to see her off, and she said you were tied up with some party."

"She was supposed to be there too, Jessie. That's what I don't understand."

"Well, she did have on that white ruffled dress of hers, but I guess that didn't mean she was planning on going to a party."

She had on that dress? I sure didn't understand that, but I said, "Oh, Jessie, she wouldn't have worn that to the mall. Didn't she say anything else?"

"Not much. Neither one of them was very talkative."

"But Middleton is too far away for just a weekend. When will they be back?"

Jessie shook her head. "I'm not sure they're coming back. They went out with the same baggage they brought in and said mail could be sent to General Delivery in Middleton. Look, kid, you must know they're hunting for Violetta's father. That's why they came to Newton Grove."

"So that's why they left." I remembered that Violetta told me her mother followed any clue. "But why did Mrs. Mills pick Middleton?"

"There was some fellow in here a while back—came in twice. She talked to him a long time but she didn't say anything to me. Only this morning she told me the guy thought he'd seen the man she described to him and she'd been thinking about it. Decided she had to check it out. What makes her think she'll find her man in Middleton anymore than she found him here, I don't know, but I guess when Selma Mills decides to pick up and move, she does it."

It was the first time I'd heard anybody call Mrs. Mills by a first name. It sounded strange.

All this time Roger stood there with his mouth hanging open. He didn't really know anything about Violetta. He was sure getting an earful now, but he didn't interrupt. I just ignored him.

"But they've got to come back," I said. "Didn't she leave a note for me or anything?"

"To tell the truth I haven't been up in the apartment since they left. Haven't had the time. It's unlocked. Why don't you go up and see? Check with me again before you go home. Let me know if you find anything."

I went up the steps two at a time with Roger close behind. Nothing was wrong with his legs—or his mouth.

"What's this all about?" he shouted. "Tell me."

"Never mind right now," I said, as I pushed the apartment door open and went in. The place looked so empty. Not that Violetta and her mother had much stuff, but it wasn't stuff that was missing. It was something else.

There was a package on the table, wrapped in birthday paper, and the card said, "For Sukie Adams." All at once I was mad at Sukie for saying what she did. Violetta really intended to go to the party, and she had bought a present. Right beside the package was an envelope with my name on it, and there was a note inside.

I didn't know we were leaving until this morning. Sorry. Please give this to Sukie. I'm glad I explained to you about my mother. She isn't going to find him in Middleton either. I think she liked it in Newton Grove. I did. I miss you already, and I haven't even left yet.

Violetta

Roger waited until I'd finished reading. Then he exploded. "Darn it, Ryker, are you going to tell me anything or not?"

"You heard Jessie," I said. "They're looking for Violetta's father. He's . . . well . . . a missing person, I guess." I didn't want to tell Roger anything else. All the stuff Violetta and I talked about I couldn't tell him. For the first time there were things I didn't want to share with Roger. I think he knew it.

"Boy," he said, "something's sure happened to you. You're not the same anymore."

I wanted to say "Likewise," but I didn't. What I did say was, "Don't be a dope. Come on, let's go."

Back downstairs we found Jessie at work again, but she took a minute to talk to us, and I told her about the note and present.

"It's a rotten deal," I said. "You told me Violetta needed a friend. Okay, she got one. Me. And I wanted her to stay here forever."

"That's life, kid. I wanted Selma to stay too. She's bright and pretty and liked by everyone. Already customers have asked for her. Maybe they'll come back. We'll just have to wait and see."

I didn't want to wait, and as Roger and I walked home I said I had to do something.

"You said you had to do something to keep Doff here too, but you couldn't come up with anything. What do you think you can do about this?"

"If I could get to Middleton . . . maybe . . . I could . . ."

"You think Violetta's mother'd listen to you?"

"No, I guess not. Why should she? I'm just a kid. I don't think she even likes me. You know, Roger, you were right. Sometimes you can't work things out without a grown-up. Mrs. Mills came to see the Judge when she first got to Newton Grove. Maybe he knows something that will help. They've just got to come back. Violetta is the first real girlfriend I've ever had. She's not like Sukie."

"You can say that again." Roger looked back over his shoulder toward Main Street. "I know how you feel, Ryker. I want Violetta to come back too. She's a neat girl."

He couldn't know how I felt. He had his folks, and Matt and Barney, and I was losing everybody.

By that time we'd come to my house and I turned in the driveway.

"I hate it, Roger. Everyone's leaving me. Doff—Violetta—"

"Well, I'm sure not going anyplace," he said. "See you tomorrow." And he headed on up the street.

Roger is a little dense sometimes.

XIX

WHEN I CAME into the house, Grandpa was in the little office he has off the living room. I don't usually bother him there, but the door was open.

I poked my head in and said, "I have to talk to you."

"Talk away," he said, putting his papers aside and looking up at me. "What's on your mind? Need a bigger allowance?"

"Oh, Grandpa, you know I can always use more money, but it's not anything like that. This is something really serious."

"Sorry, honey. Time was, though, you thought a bigger allowance was pretty serious business. Forgive me." He pointed to the chair across from him at the desk. "Sit down."

He was treating me like a grown-up and I liked it.

"So," he said, "is it Doff you want to talk about?"

"It isn't about Doff either. It's about my friend, Violetta Mills, and her mother."

"Yes?"

"They've gone away."

"Oh," he said, "I hadn't heard that."

"Just this morning—to Middleton." And I told him what happened and that I knew about Mrs. Mills looking for Violetta's father and that that was why they came to Newton Grove.

Grandpa nodded. "I guess everybody in town knows that by now."

"I know about the picture in the paper too."

I think that surprised him. He raised his eyebrows and said, "You seem to know the whole story. The picture was taken outside my courtroom all right, but the fellow she pointed out to me was Dan Steuben's brother, Henry. Just in town for a visit. The case we had that day was of some political interest and the *Sentinel* sent over a photographer. Henry happened to get in the background."

"The thing is, Grandpa, I want them to come back. I thought maybe you might know something that would help."

"I'm afraid I don't have any special information." He frowned and ran his fingers over his chin. "Mrs. Mills and I didn't talk long. I told her Henry Steuben had lived in Calverson all his life, had a wife and four children. That was about it. When I asked when she'd seen her husband last she cut me off, said to forget it and left. I was sorry I couldn't be of any assistance. Perhaps Middleton was a good lead."

"But they've been looking so long." And I told him what Violetta had said about her father's leaving.

That must have been something Grandpa didn't know, because he said, "Hmm," and then sat there for a few minutes just tapping his fingers on the top of his desk—thinking, I guess. Finally, he said, "Well, that does put a different light on the matter. Just between you and me, honey, they may never find him. Twelve years is a long time."

"Violetta doesn't think they will. But they're gone—off to Middleton and who knows where else, maybe far away. Violetta is my very best friend now, and I don't want to lose her."

"I see." Grandpa was rubbing his chin again. At least he was listening to me. "Honestly, Amy," he said, "I'm not sure there's anything I can do."

I moved forward in the chair and laid my hands flat on the desk the way I'd seen him do when he had a plan. "Well, I've thought of something," I said. "We could go to Middleton and you could tell Mrs. Mills she has to come back. She won't care what I say, but you're important, and if you're the one who . . ."

"Hold on now. Your friend's mother might not welcome my interference."

That was true, but I didn't care. "Then at least," I said, "we could write a letter."

Grandpa leaned back in his chair and nodded. "Now that's a possibility."

"Sure." I was getting excited about the idea. And to think the Judge was going along with it. "We could write and tell her that if Middleton turned out to be another goose chase, they should come back to Newton Grove and if there was ever any news about Violetta's father you'd see she got it."

Grandpa was still nodding, and I could tell he was thinking it out. "Yes," he said. "We could write a letter like that. And we'll do it now." He pulled paper from his desk and picked up a pen.

Boy, when the Judge decides to do something, he gets right to it.

It took him only a few minutes, and I sat there across from him while he wrote. When he finished, he handed the letter to me.

"Does it meet with your approval?" he said. "Have we made our point?"

It was a super letter. Grandpa not only said what I asked him to, he said more—that he would see what he could find out about Violetta's father through Washington. If he'd ever been in the military there would be records. Or there might be some other lead. The letter was so great I decided if I ever had to find somebody, I'd come straight to the Judge.

When the envelope was sealed and stamped, I had another idea. "Wouldn't it be good," I said, "if Jessie wrote too? She could tell Mrs. Mills she needed her at the restaurant. She really does, you know."

"It will certainly do no harm."

"We could go downtown right now and ask her, and if she'll do it we can get both letters off tonight."

This time Grandpa didn't have to answer. He was on his feet.

At the restaurant, Jessie was all for the idea. "Only thing," she said, "I'm not much good at letters."

"That doesn't matter," I said. I reached over the counter for one of her menus. "Just write it here. Tell her you want her back."

And that's the way it worked out. The Judge and I took the

letters straight to the post office and he let me drop them in the slot.

"After all, it's your project," he said. "Good luck. I hope it works."

"Thank you, Grandpa."

"At any rate, honey, we've done what we could. Now we'll just have to wait and see."

That was just what Jessie said, but this time I couldn't think of anything else to do.

As we left the post office, Grandpa took my arm. "Now that our business is taken care of, Miss Ryker, let's go back to Jessie's for a hamburger. Then I suggest we take in a movie."

How about that? It was the very thing Violetta had done with her mother their first night in town.

XX

VIOLETTA'S MOTHER would probably get the letters by Tuesday. She might not answer, of course, but I wasn't going to think about that.

Anyhow, Grandpa and I had a great time on Saturday night, and then on Sunday afternoon we went to the Enslows for an early dinner. Only thing, Roger wasn't going to be there. As a matter of fact, he was on his way out the door as we went in.

Mrs. Enslow said he'd made plans last month to go to some sports show in Calverson with Matt and his dad.

"I told him I knew you'd understand," she said, "and I'm sure he's sorry not to be home, since you're here."

He didn't look very sorry as he sailed down the front walk, but I did understand. It meant, though, I didn't get a chance to tell him about sending the letters to Middleton. That would have to wait until tomorrow.

It was funny sitting at the dining room table with Roger's parents and no Roger. Still, it was a good dinner. Mrs. Enslow fixed everything I like, from cheese potatoes to pumpkin pie. I think she was the one who was sorry.

After dinner the Enslows and the Judge went into the living room to talk, and I had the TV in the den all to myself. I didn't have to argue with Roger about what program to watch. The trouble was I couldn't get interested in anything. I felt lonely.

We didn't stay very late. The Judge had some papers to go over, he said, and by seven we were back home. He went into his office and I went upstairs to finish a little homework I'd put off all weekend. I was getting used to having just the two of us in the house.

The next morning, it was back to school, and on the way I told Roger about the letters. It would have been better if I'd just kept still, because he didn't think they'd do any good. "Nah," he said, "it's too bad but she's gone."

"Don't say that. Don't even think it," I said. "And if that's the way you feel, let's not talk about it."

When Violetta didn't show up in class, Miss Pritchett asked me if I knew why she was absent.

"I'm sorry," I said. "I haven't seen Violetta since Friday." That was true, and I didn't want to tell the rest. Word would get around soon enough.

I'd brought the package for Sukie, and I think she was a little embarrassed to take it.

"Go ahead," I said. "It's yours." I didn't need to twist her arm.

The present was a gold chain bracelet, and I could see Sukie liked it. She should. It probably took all of the money Violetta had saved from her odd jobs for Jessie.

"If you see her," Sukie said, "tell her thanks."

"I just delivered it," I snapped. "When she comes back, you tell her. You owe her."

That was Monday. On Tuesday, real early, we got a phone call from Doff. We'd expected her to get home that afternoon, but she said she wouldn't be able to make it until Thursday. She wasn't sure what time. She was getting a ride from a friend of her friend. He had business in Calverson and would drop her off here on his way. She didn't say anything about when she was leaving for England, only that she was anxious to get back to us. Maybe since she was staying a couple of extra days with her friend in the city, she'd stay a little longer in Newton Grove to make up for it. I'd ask her.

Also by Tuesday I was sure Miss Pritchett knew about Violetta and her mother, but I don't think she would have said anything if Sukie hadn't raised her hand and asked if the new girl was ever coming back.

"I certainly hope so," she told her, "but if she doesn't we'll all miss her. Maybe she's just out of town for a few days."

Nobody would miss her like I would, but at lunchtime Kimberly and several of the other girls did tell me they liked having Violetta in class and were sorry she was gone.

Of course I hoped the letters would bring her back, and I wondered if they'd gotten there yet. And if they had, how soon would Mrs. Mills go to the post office to pick them up? Maybe she didn't expect to get mail right away. Maybe she'd wait a few days before checking.

Wait! I was beginning to hate that word.

One good thing. We were real busy at school getting ready for the Pumpkin Faire on Saturday. They wouldn't start decorating Main Street until Friday, but we had a lot to do for open house before that—putting our work up on the blackboards, making welcome signs for all over the place, and most important, secretly, or not so secretly, planning for our contest entries.

Sukie never told anybody anything about hers, which was funny since she couldn't keep other people's secrets for a minute.

Roger and I had always told each other what we had in mind, but this year he said he'd need a lot of help because of his arm, and he and Barney and Matt were doing something together. That was okay. I suppose it would be hard for Roger when he still had that stupid cast, but I could have helped him. He also told me he didn't mind if I knew what their idea was, but Barney said, "Tell anybody and you're dead."

Anyhow, on Wednesday right after school, I hiked out by myself to Larkin's farm to pick out my pumpkin. Mr. Larkin always lets us roam his field until we find what we want, and I really lucked out. A white one, about the size of a real head and not too round.

I'd found a good picture of Mary Poppins in one of my books, and after dinner I took all the stuff out to the service porch and set to work. The book said she had black shiny hair, and I had found half a ball of black yarn in the scrap drawer. I draped strands of it across the top of the pumpkin and down the sides. Then I pulled them into a little knot at the back. It was the face that gave me trouble. I couldn't get the eyes right, and I finally gave up at eight-thirty. There was still tomorrow. We were to bring the pumpkins in on Friday. Mrs. Clement, the librarian, was in charge of the contest, and she and the teachers would stay on in the afternoon to set things up.

Not many of the little kids bring anything, but last year we must have had over fifty entries from the fourth, fifth, and sixth grades alone. That's a lot of pumpkins.

On Thursday morning before he left for town, Grandpa took out one of the casseroles and three of the apple tarts Doff had left in the freezer for us.

"Just in case she gets here in time for dinner," he said. "I'll try to get home early."

At lunch, Sukie wound up eating in the cafeteria with me. "It's too bad," she said, "that your friend isn't going to be here for the Faire. You know I don't think she's out of town for a few days at all. I think she's gone for good."

I wanted to tell her I didn't care what she thought. I had certainly hoped Violetta would be here, and I wondered what was happening in Middleton. Suppose Violetta and the Judge were wrong and Mr. Mills had been found. Suppose Violetta was already in another school. Suppose she was gone for good. I was worried, but I wasn't going to admit it to Sukie.

I left school alone. Roger was going to Matt's and was even planning to spend the night. Anyhow, I hurried home to finish Mary Poppins. I wanted it to be ready when Doff got there, to see what she thought of it. I tried the face again, and this time it wasn't too bad—small blue eyes, a straight mouth and little circles of pink on the cheeks. When I set that wonderful hat square on top and tied my white scarf around her neck, she looked pretty good. Not great but good. I had the umbrella too, but I didn't know what to do with it. I'd decide in the morning.

Grandpa did get home early and we put the casserole in the oven at five-thirty. Allowing an hour for it to bake, we figured Doff might get there. I set the table for three and we hoped for the best.

She didn't make it. We were down to dessert when there was another call from her. I was the one who picked up the phone, and as soon as I heard her voice, I said, "Where are you? We thought you'd be here by now."

"I'm so sorry, Luv. That's why I'm calling. We've had car trouble. They told us it might take awhile before we'll be on our way again, and we're still a good three hours from Newton Grove. I'll be late. Is the Judge at hand?"

"Sure," I said and gave him the phone.

They talked for a few minutes. He asked if she had a good visit and how was the weather. Then he said, "Oh, that soon?" and "No problem at all." and finally, "Don't worry. We'll expect you when we see you. Good luck."

When we went back to the table, he said, "Well, she's taken care of everything. Has her plane reservation to New York and on to London. She'll be leaving from the city on Sunday night."

"Sunday?" I said. "This Sunday? That's in three days."

"At least she'll spend those days with us. We'll take her back to the city for her flight."

My throat kind of closed up. I looked down at the rest of the apple tart on my plate and knew I couldn't swallow another bite.

"Excuse me, Grandpa," I said. "I don't think I can eat any

more, and do you mind if we wait awhile to clean up the kitchen. I don't feel very good."

"I understand, honey. I'll take care of things."

It was no lie. I felt terrible. She had her reservations. There wouldn't even be any extra days. I just wanted to be alone, and I went upstairs and down the hall.

Doff's room is across from mine and the door was wide open. That's the way she usually leaves it. I'd never gone in when she wasn't there, but tonight it seemed to be okay.

Right away I smelled the lilac. It was the smell Doff always had around her, and maybe that was the reason the room didn't feel empty and cold like Violetta's apartment had. It was still filled with Doff. Her hand mirror was on the dressing table along with her mother's picture and the little jewel box I'd given her one Christmas. The book she was reading was on the nightstand and beside it was a pen and notepad. I'd seen all these things lots of times. They belonged there. But there were things in the room that didn't belong there at all. Two large suitcases, which must have been brought down from the attic, were standing by the wardrobe closet, and several packing boxes were lined up against the wall. I went over to look at them. A couple were labeled "For the Salvation Army," and a couple more "To Be Sent to Me When There's Time." I guess I knew she'd been packing but I hadn't watched her do it.

One familiar thing did look wrong though. Her blue wing chair over by the window. She should be sitting in it. I'd missed her these last days, but now I thought how awful it would be when she was really gone. Way down inside of me was a terrible ache. My eyes blurred over like they did the night she told me she was leaving, and for once I wished I was a crier. Maybe tears would help.

I couldn't stand to see that chair empty, and I curled up in it and closed my eyes.

When I woke up Grandpa was standing beside me, gently patting me on the arm.

"It's past bedtime, Amy. Tomorrow is a school day. Doff won't get home until eleven or so, but you'll see her in the morning."

I looked over at the little crystal clock on the bedside table. A quarter to ten. It was really past bedtime. I was still half asleep, but I grunted an "Okay" and stumbled across the hall to bed.

XXI

IT WAS THE SMELL of Doff's blueberry muffins that woke me up on Friday morning. I dressed in record time and tore downstairs. There she was at the stove just as though she'd never been away.

"Oh, Doff," I said, "I'm so glad to have you home."

"It's good to be here, Luv." Then she gave me a soft sad look. "Even if it's only to go away again. I hope you're ready to forgive me for that."

"Just don't talk about it." I plopped down in my chair at the breakfast table, and since I was a little early she joined me, bringing her coffee cup along with her.

"The Judge is already on his way to town," she said. "This is going to be a busy day for us all. I took a peek at your Mary Poppins out there on the porch. She's lovely."

"Thanks, but I don't know what to do about the umbrella.

I can't have her holding it high above her head the way it ought to be if she's floating down from the sky. No arms."

"True, but I have an idea. Why don't you set her on that square pastry board of mine and lay the umbrella unopened alongside. Also, I have a pair of white gloves you can have. She always wore gloves. You can put those with the umbrella and your Mary Poppins will be perfect."

"That's good," I said. "I didn't even think about the gloves."

While I finished breakfast, she put everything out for me, and all that was left to do was pack it up to carry to school. The board, the pumpkin head, and the gloves fit into a large shopping bag. The umbrella I tucked under my arm. I had my book bag too, but that goes on my back. I was loaded down, but I got everything there all right.

Sometime during the past two weeks everybody who was entering the contest was supposed to bring in a big cardboard carton to hold his entry, and these were already lined up in the gym with our names on them. I found mind right away and there next to it was Violetta's. It gave me a funny feeling. I just put my shopping bag and the umbrella in my carton, didn't bother to set it up. Then I stopped by the library and explained to Mrs. Clement how it was to be. She said she'd take care of it.

Naturally, everybody was late getting into the classroom. Roger, Matt, and Barney came in together. I guess Barney had stayed all night at Matt's too. Anyhow, when Roger slid into his seat across the aisle he said Matt's mother brought their entry in for them. He still wouldn't tell me what it was.

It was almost ten o'clock before Sukie arrived all out of breath.

"Mother brought me to school," she said, "and we went straight to the library with my pumpkin. Mrs. Clement said it was very creative. I just bet anything I'll win."

She didn't tell me what she'd come up with either, but I didn't care. By tomorrow there'd be no secrets.

There was so much excitement about the Faire it was hard to be serious about schoolwork. Miss Pritchett knew it and she had us read *The Legend of Sleepy Hollow* like we did *The Incredible Journey,* taking turns around the class. Then she told us ghost stories. Since we can't get it pitch dark in our room in the daytime, she said to close our eyes real tight and pretend it was midnight. Boy, everybody should have a teacher like Miss Pritchett.

It was a good day, but I did miss Violetta, especially after school when I saw Roger head off toward town with his friends and I was alone again. I was anxious to get home, though. Doff didn't know any of the stuff about Violetta. I hadn't started on that this morning. There was too much to tell.

I found her in her room emptying out drawers and sorting things that still had to be boxed. She kept right on working while we talked.

"I am so sorry to hear about Violetta," she said when she heard the story, "but this is only Friday, hardly time to expect a response from your letters. Just hold the thought that she will come back."

"Holding thoughts isn't keeping you here," I said, and I'm sure I sounded cross.

"I know you're angry because I'm leaving, Amy. I'm a little angry myself. I've even thought how nice it would be if I could take you with me, but I don't have the right to do that. All I can hope is that we will somehow one day get together again, but I can't even promise that, can I?"

She stopped in her work long enough to take a little package from the top of the dresser. "I have a small gift for you, Amy. I hope you like it."

We sat down on the bed together and I opened the box. It was a jewel case and inside there was an old-fashioned locket. I knew before I opened the locket that there would be a picture of her. That was very special, because Doff never, ever, has her picture taken. She says it's against her principles.

"When did you do this?" I asked. "I can't believe it."

"In the city, Luv. Just this week. I know you're laughing at me, but this is one time a picture is important. I don't want you to forget my face."

"How could I?" I said, and I kind of choked up. "I love you." I don't remember ever saying that to her before.

"And I love you, my dear. No matter where I am." She folded her arms around me, and I smelled the lilac. Then we sat there for a few minutes without saying anything. It was the second time in two days I wished I was a crier.

All at once she looked at her watch. "My goodness, it's getting late. I intended to fix a special dinner for tonight, but the Judge said I was absolutely not to cook, that we would go to Jessie's, and I guess I'll have to do as he says. He plans to be home a little early, and I'll never be ready in time if I don't hurry. Why don't you get another carton, Amy, and give me a hand."

It was good to be busy and we worked for another half hour together before we stopped to change clothes for dinner.

Grandpa had told Jessie we'd be at the restaurant about six, and she was waiting for us at the door. She had decorated her place for the Faire like she always does, and there were cornstalks and pumpkins all over.

"If I had a red carpet I'd have rolled it out," she said, as she took both of Doff's hands in hers. "This is a special night. I'm not sure Jessie's kitchen can compete with yours, but I'll give it my best shot. You just tell me what you'll have."

She led us to a table by the front window and handed us her menus.

I had too much on my mind to be excited about food. That's not normal for me, but we all ordered the roast chicken and Doff said it was especially good. Like I told Violetta back when she first came here, Jessie's is the best place in town.

We talked while we ate. Jessie wondered if the mall would be completely deserted over the weekend with everybody coming downtown, and Grandpa said, "There's a lot of ill feeling about the chain shops out there, but in a way it's too bad they're too far away to take part in the Main Street festivities. The Faire's a town tradition, and we're not about to give it up."

Then we got onto the subject of the open house and the contest. Grandpa said he'd checked out my Mary Poppins before he left the house and thought it was a success.

Doff wanted to know who was doing the judging this year, and I told her Miss Nordoff from the town library, Mr. Steuben, and I thought they got old Mr. Hedges, the bank president.

"They try to get people not connected with the school," I said, "people who wouldn't know who the entries belonged to."

"That's the way it should be," she agreed. "and when do they announce the winners?"

"Well," I said, "the judges usually come when the doors first open in the morning, and as soon as they turn in their votes, the names are posted on the bulletin board just inside the office."

"No question," said Grandpa, "it will be unanimous for Amy Ryker."

"Oh, sure," I said, and we all laughed.

It was a kind of sad-glad dinner. I don't think any of us wanted to mention that Doff would be leaving in only two days, but finally she was the one who brought it up.

"You're sure it won't be a problem to drive me back to the city on Sunday," she said. "It seems a little unfair since you took me there once already."

"Not at all," insisted Grandpa. "We'll make an outing of it, and this time Amy won't get left behind. You say your plane takes off for New York at three, and I figure if we leave here about eight in the morning we can see you on your way and get back to Newton Grove the same day."

Doff said she certainly appreciated it.

I didn't say anything. How could I with this gloom hanging over me?

Jessie had waited on us herself and when we got down to dessert she wanted to know if everything had been all right.

"Everything was excellent," said Grandpa. "Why don't you sit down with us and have a piece of this lemon pie. I highly recommend it."

To be honest, I was getting itchy. We'd been sitting there a long time. I was glad when Jessie said she'd take a rain check.

"There'll be a rush when the eastbound bus arrives," she said, "and it's due any minute." She glanced at her watch and then out to the street. "What did I tell you," she said. "Right on time, and it's full."

I looked out the window to see the bus pull up to the station just beyond Jessie's door. It sure was full, and I watched people step down onto the curb. An old man with a beard and a briefcase, a bunch of ladies with almost the same kind of hats, a woman carrying a baby and behind her a girl with . . .

"Hey," I screamed. "That's Violetta. She's back."

And without bothering to grab my jacket I ran for the door.

XXII

THERE SHE WAS all right, standing at the curb with her mother. They were waiting for the driver to unload the baggage, and Violetta was facing away from me.

"Hi," I said, and when she turned around I saw that under her coat she was wearing the white dress. "I'm the welcoming committee."

Those blue eyes sort of lit up. "Amy," she said, "what are you doing here? I didn't expect you to be the first person I'd see."

"Aren't you glad I am?"

"Sure—of course—you know that."

I think she was as excited as I was but she seemed a little nervous, and she glanced over at her mother.

Mrs. Mills was pointing out their suitcases to the driver, and when she had them in hand she turned around too. Her hair was pulled back the same way she always wore it, but she had on a blue suit and high heels. It was funny. She seemed more—well—grown up.

"Mother," said Violetta, "see who's here—Amy."

And Mrs. Mills surprised me when she said, "Hello, Amy," and really looked at me.

I told them the Judge and Doff and I were just finishing dinner. "Come on." I led them inside and over to the table.

"I guess everybody knows everybody," I said.

Doff nodded and smiled, and Grandpa stood up and pulled over another chair.

"I'm pleased that you chose to return to Newton Grove," he said. "Why don't you join us? Have you had dinner?"

"Oh, yes," said Mrs. Mills. "The bus driver gave us a food break. We've eaten." She smiled too, and it was a good smile.

"At least," said Doff, "have a cup of coffee with us."

Mrs. Mills took the chair Grandpa held out for her and Jessie signaled for Ruthie to bring another cup to the table.

"Well, Selma," said Jessie, "are you ready to come back to work? We've sure missed you around here."

"That's what you wrote to me," said Violetta's mother, and she looked so pleased. "I missed you too." Then she turned to Grandpa. "And thank you, Judge Ryker. Letta says you make sense."

"I try," he said. "Why don't you come to the house one day next week and we'll talk."

"For now," said Jessie, "your apartment is still upstairs waiting for you. It's just as you left it. I haven't even taken your name off the door."

This was all beautiful, but I wanted to get away alone with Violetta.

"Why don't we take your bags upstairs," I said, and since nobody seemed to mind we left.

The apartment was still unlocked and as soon as we got inside, I said, "There is so much for you to tell me, but first off, you're wearing that white dress again, and Jessie told me you had it on when you left. How come?"

She flipped her hair back in that old way. "I told you I like ruffles and pink ribbon. Doesn't that answer your question?"

She was teasing me, and I said, "No, it doesn't. Come on."

"All right," and she was suddenly serious, "you might as well know, Amy. It's my trouble dress. I wear it when things aren't going right or I'm not sure they will. It makes me feel better. I really do like ruffles."

Boy, I felt so guilty. Something must have happened in Middleton, and I wasn't giving her a chance to tell me.

"I'm sorry," I said. "I should have asked you right away about your father. I guess you wouldn't be here if you found him, but was there any news?"

"Of course there wasn't. I knew there wouldn't be. Oh, we talked to the man who was supposed to look like my father, but Mother said he didn't—not at all. Besides, he'd been in Middleton for fifteen years, owns a hardware store there. I told you before, it's all so stupid."

While we were talking, Violetta had gone over to the dresser and pulled something from behind it. I saw now that it was a picture, the picture of her father.

"How did that get there?" I asked.

"I put it there," she said. "I hoped maybe she'd want it bad enough to come back for it. It's so important to her. She thinks we forgot to pack it, but I purposely left it behind."

"And *was* that the reason she came back?"

"I don't think so. At least not the most important reason. My mother hasn't given up on finding my father, but she did admit to me that Middleton was a waste of time. Then when the Judge wrote that he'd help—well—she thinks he's a smart man."

"I could have told her that."

"Besides, Jessie said she needed her. I don't think anybody's ever said that to my mother before. No, it was the letters. And I'll bet they were your idea, weren't they?"

I nodded and she said, "Thanks."

"Anyhow," I said, "now that you're here, are you going to stay?"

She shrugged. "Who knows? This is the first time we've ever gone back to a place once we left, but all the same, we'll have to wait and see."

There were those words again—for the third time, and I still didn't like them. I might as well change the subject, and I said, "Well, don't forget we've got the Faire tomorrow. How about your pumpkin head? You took a carton to school, and it's still there. Did you ever decide what you were going to do?"

"Not really. I thought about it, but what was the use?"

"You can still get something ready. Jessie has all those pumpkins. She'd give you one and you could call Mrs. Clement . . ."

"Hold it, Amy. You are impossible. Why would I want to go to all that trouble?"

"Because you're part of our class, that's why."

"I've never been a part of that class. You know it."

"That's not true. Miss Pritchett said she hoped you'd come back, and if you didn't we'd all miss you."

"And I'm sure Sukie cried her eyes out because I was gone."

"You can't count Sukie. She's the one who doesn't belong to the class. A lot of people said they like having you here. Roger even said you were a neat girl."

I don't know what she would have said about that, because right then Doff's voice floated up the stairs.

"It's time to go, Amy. Tomorrow is a big day."

"Okay," I called back. "Just a minute."

Violetta had opened one of the suitcases, hers I guess, and began taking things out. How weird it would be to have everything you own in a single bag. And again I had the thought I'd had a lot these past weeks. Violetta Mills was some special person.

"Anyhow," I said, "I'm one of the greeters at school tomorrow. From ten until noon—the whole time. I'll see you there."

"Maybe."

"Come on. You've got to see my Mary Poppins. Besides, Miss Pritchett has your art work and your test papers hung up all over the room. You'll want to show them to your mother."

"She may be working."

"Even if she is you know Jessie will let her off for an hour. Jessie even comes herself."

"I won't promise."

This time it was Grandpa's voice that shot up the stairway. "We're waiting, Amy. Snap to it."

There is something about the Judge's voice that demands action, and I said, "Coming, Grandpa. Right away." And to Violetta I said, "I'm sure glad you're back."

When we got home I headed straight for the phone. I had to tell Roger the news.

It was Dr. Enslow who answered. "Roger is spending the night with Matt again, Amy. You can reach him there if you want. Do you have the number?"

"Thanks, but I won't bother him," I said. "He'll be at the school tomorrow."

Chalk that up. One more time Roger wasn't there when I wanted him.

XXIII

MY ALARM WAS set for eight, but I was up half an hour before it went off. I could hardly wait to get to school. Of course, Doff insisted I eat a good breakfast. "Because," she said, "you'll probably fill yourself with all sorts of unnourishing things before the day is over."

She was right about that. I did the best I could with the cream of wheat and took a banana to eat along the way.

Open house didn't begin until ten, but Mr. Anderberry said the student hosts could come earlier so they could see the pumpkin display before they had to report to their classrooms.

By earlier, I think he meant nine-thirty, but I was there before that. Except for the teachers, I think I was the first. Even though the front door was locked, we could come in at the back of the gym and from there into the main building.

I wanted to see the pumpkins, of course, but more important

I wanted to break the news about Violetta. I hadn't been able to tell Roger, but I could tell Miss Pritchett. I was sure she'd be here already, and wouldn't she be surprised. I wasted no time crossing the gym floor and dashed up the stairs and down the hall to the sixth-grade room.

The thing was, I got the surprise. Miss Pritchett was there all right, but with her arm around Violetta. Besides, guess what? Violetta was in pants and a sweater—no white dress.

Miss Pritchett said, "Good morning, Amy, and look who's come back in time for the Faire."

"I know," I said. "I was coming to tell you."

Violetta winked at me, and Miss Pritchett said, "Not only is she back, she brought an entry for the contest."

"Amy said I should," said Violetta quickly. "I thought it would be too late, but she said no."

"It certainly isn't too late," said Miss Pritchett. "I'll take it down to Mrs. Clement myself and see that it's set up and properly labeled."

That was when I noticed the big paper bag on the desk. I was dying to peek inside. What had she come up with? But Miss Pritchett gathered it in her arms and said, "Why don't you girls go downstairs and look around. There are some wonderfully original entries. You have plenty of time. Just get back here by ten. You can be a room hostess too, Violetta. We can always use another." And off she went.

"So you did bring a pumpkin, after all," I said, as we ran down the stairs. "Is it what you'd planned on in the beginning?"

"No, the idea just came to me."

"What is it?"

"You'll see," she said, and that was all I could get out of her.

A few other kids had come in by then. They'd asked maybe two or three student greeters for each class. Altogether there'd be about fifteen. Sukie was the other one for our room, but she's always late.

Tables had been set up along one side of the first floor hallway, and the entries, arranged by grades, had name cards with them and sometimes titles. Like I said, no secrets now.

I wanted to find the sixth-grade table right away, but Violetta pulled me back.

"Let's just go down the hall," she said, "and take the grades as we come to them. We'll get to ours soon enough."

I gave in, and, of course, if we started at one end and worked our way down, we wouldn't miss anything.

There were more pumpkins from the kindergarten and first grade than I expected, but I had a feeling parents had a hand in most of them. There were a couple of the seven dwarfs—Doc and Dopey—and there was a wonderful Captain Hook. No little kid could have done those faces. I guess help was allowed, though, for the lower grades.

It would take all day to tell you everything that was there. Witches and ghosts and pirates. There was a monster with bulging eyes and sharp teeth, Ernie from Sesame Street, a plain mouse, a Mickey Mouse, and a couple of Ninja Turtles.

Finally, we did get to the sixth-grade table at the end of the hall. I took a quick look around trying to spot something Violetta might have thought up just overnight. I couldn't even find her name.

"Okay, where is it?" I asked.

"I don't know," she said. "Probably not out here yet. But your Mary Poppins is terrific."

"Thank you. I don't really expect it to win, but it does look all right, and Mrs. Clement set it up just the way I asked."

While I was checking it out, Violetta moved on.

"Here's Roger's" she said, pointing to three pumpkins all the same size. Of course, it was Barney's and Matt's too, and it was a clever idea. "SEE NO EVIL, HEAR NO EVIL, SPEAK NO EVIL." But they weren't monkeys. Instead, they'd given them stocking caps and fastened mittens over the eyes of one, the ears of the second, and the mouth of the third. I could tell which was Roger's because painting a face with your left hand isn't easy, and SEE NO EVIL looked a little ragged. At least he didn't have to do eyes, which are the hardest.

Finding Sukie's was no problem at all—a kid with measles, an ice bag on her head, a thermometer in her round painted mouth, and red spots all over. Really good, I had to admit, and the perfect idea for sick-in-bed-all-the-time Sukie.

The twins did separate things this year, both babies though, one with a bonnet and pacifier, the other with a bottle and a bib. Both had ribbons tied to the stems which were supposed to look like locks of hair.

"And would you look at this one," I shouted. "It's Kimberly Todd's. Super, and I didn't even know she brought anything."

The card said, "CINDERELLA AFTER MIDNIGHT," and the huge pumpkin had been carefully carved into a coach with side windows and a door. Six toy mice were lined up as horses, and a rubber rat, the coachman, sat on top in a wooden driver's seat and held the reins. Leaning out the window was Cinderella herself, a Barbie doll dressed in rags and with her hair in a tangle.

"I bet on this one for a winner," said Violetta. "The carving alone is worth a prize. That must have been tricky."

I was getting impatient. It was almost ten o'clock. "Okay," I said, "now where *is* yours?"

Almost as soon as I said it, I saw Mrs. Clement come up with Violetta's entry. That was what she had to be carrying, and she made room for it at the end of the table.

The pumpkin was completely wrapped in strips of white cloth like a mummy. There was a man's felt hat on top with the brim pulled down a little. A pair of dark-rimmed glasses covered two eyeholes and was perched over a hump under the wrapping—the nose, of course. There was a pipe sticking out of a slit in the cloth right where the mouth would be, and tied around the bottom was a brown wool muffler.

I didn't need to look at the card Mrs. Clement propped against the entry. I knew what it was. "THE INVISIBLE MAN."

XXIV

"THE INVISIBLE MAN." I knew where Violetta got that idea. And she knew I knew. She looked over at me and grinned. All at once it was very funny, and we both started to laugh.

Mrs. Clement had gone back into the library and Violetta leaned close to me and whispered, "Not finding my father isn't really a sad thing, you know. I didn't expect to, and I haven't any feelings about him at all."

Just then the front doors of the school were pushed open, and there were shouts and a scurry of feet as people came rushing into the building.

"We'd better go back upstairs," I said. "Miss Pritchett may need us."

On the way Violetta said, "Well, what do you think?"

"You mean about your pumpkin? I think you might win.

As far as I know, nobody's done The Invisible Man before. But what did your mother say?"

"Oh, she didn't connect it to my father. She said she liked it and even borrowed the pipe from Ben for me."

That's all we had time for. Miss Pritchett was motioning us to hurry.

There isn't a lot to do as greeters. Most of the parents come with their kids who do their own showing around, but we're there to answer questions or just smile.

Almost right away Jessie came in with Violetta's mother.

"Ben and Ruthie are minding the store," said Jessie, "but we can't stay very long. Main Street's already bustling."

Violetta's mother was in the blue suit again. Nice. She looked carefully at everything Violetta showed her, and I heard her say, "I'm proud of you, Letta."

I asked her if they'd seen the pumpkins yet, but she said they'd look at them on their way out. "And I'll be sure to find yours, Amy. Letta told me about it."

Boy, she was sure friendlier than she was before.

Sukie finally turned up at ten-thirty, and I said, "I thought you were supposed to be here early."

"I had to wait for Mother." That's Sukie, always blaming somebody else.

"Anyhow," she said, "it looks as though you have someone to take my place, so why are you complaining?" She sort of sniffed in Violetta's direction and hurried her mother over to see our goldfish and a guinea pig we've been keeping since school started. When Mrs. Adams went downstairs, Sukie did stay to help us, though, which was good because she's in charge of the goldfish.

149

The Enslows drifted in at about eleven with Roger. I didn't have to tell him about Violetta being back. He saw her. His eyes popped, and he lifted his good hand in greeting. He didn't do anything silly, though. After all, his folks were there.

Doff and the Judge arrived a few minutes after the Enslows, and I took over with them. They always want to see what I've done, and I had a few things on the wall—tests and drawings—and my workbook was on my desk. They were going to check out the pumpkins on their way out too. They said they'd see me later down on Main Street.

A lot of people came into our room, even some of the lower grade parents. I guess they were interested in the whole school. Mr. Leatherman said, "Time goes so fast. It won't be long before our baby will be moving upstairs." And he laughed. Patsy Leatherman is in first grade.

The morning went fast anyway. It was a quarter to twelve before we knew it. Sukie had already asked if she could go down and find her mother, and Miss Pritchett said since no one else seemed to be coming, we could go too if we wanted to.

"I'm sure the contest winners will be posted by now. Run along. If I don't see you downtown during the afternoon, I'll see you bright and early Monday morning. Have a good time."

Once again Violetta and I dashed down the stairs, but there was such a mob around the office we couldn't get anywhere near it.

All at once we heard Mr. Anderberry's voice over the loud-speaker. He must have figured this might happen.

"With the permission of the judges," he said, "I'd like to announce the winners for each grade." He started rattling off names, beginning with the kindergarten. They had a first and second place, so it took a few minutes and Violetta and I just stood there waiting for him to get to us.

When he finally did, he cleared his throat and said, "The judges tell me Miss Pritchett's room was the most difficult. There were so many delightful entries. However, in first place we have CINDERELLA AFTER MIDNIGHT, which was submitted by Kimberly Todd. I've seen it myself, and I'm in agreement. Very clever, very well executed."

There was a lot of clapping. I looked over at Kimberly, and she had her hands over her face as if she didn't believe it. Kimberly's okay. I didn't really expect to win anyhow, and I was happy for her.

Mr. Anderberry called for quiet and then said, "And in second place we have THE INVISIBLE MAN by Violetta Mills." Again there was clapping and a lot of shouting from the boys. In the middle of it was Matt's whistle.

After the announcements, the crowd moved away from the office and the winners could go in and pick up their prizes. They aren't that big. Ten dollars for first and five for second. It was the winning that counted. Besides, those who got the money usually went right down to Main Street and spent it.

I saw Sukie go out the door with her mother. MEASLES didn't get a prize after all, and I think she was a little mad.

At noon the open house was over. People still hung around for awhile, but as soon as everybody was out, the building would be locked. The pumpkins could be picked up and taken home if the kids were in a hurry to get them back. Otherwise, everything would be left as it was until Monday.

Most of the crowd would wind up down on Main Street

pretty soon, especially the school kids. I wanted Violetta to myself though, and I tried to keep us away from the others. There were still things we hadn't talked about. She didn't know that Doff was leaving on Sunday, and when I told her she said, "That came up fast, didn't it? What are you and the Judge going to do?"

"I don't know. I can't bear the thought of anybody else in Doff's room. I told you what Mrs. Jenkins was like, and then there was that awful Mrs. Honeycut."

"Maybe there doesn't have to be anybody. Did you ever think of that?"

"You mean Grandpa and I could just manage alone . . . ? By ourselves?"

"Why not? You did it for a week."

"But I told you how that was, with Doff leaving everything ready for us."

Violetta shrugged. "The Judge could hire someone to wash and clean for you. Couldn't you two take care of meals?"

"I don't know whether Grandpa can cook, but I've never done any more than open a can of soup."

"So what? You don't have to worry about money. You could even eat out all the time."

Boy, I couldn't imagine the Judge going for that. I just shook my head. "I don't know."

We came onto Main Street, down at the far end where they always hold the Saturday market. It had been dark last night when we went to Jessie's so I hadn't seen how they decorated. All up and down the street were orange and yellow and green streamers draped from one lamppost to another, and the same color balloons were tied to every tree. But the smell of things was the best. First of all there was the smoker wagon that Mr. Walchek brings to town on special days, and if you haven't smelled Walchek's smoked ribs you've missed something. Today, besides the ribs, he had ham, sausages, pork chops. You could take home whatever you wanted, or you could have sandwiches right on the spot, because Mrs. Walchek was there beside the wagon with her fresh-baked bread.

All the farmers had their garden stuff same as always, but for the Faire they brought more than that. Portable barbecues were set up for chicken and sweet corn. Pots of bean soup and stew bubbled away on camp stoves. There were tamales and enchiladas and all kinds of baked stuff. Mrs. Quinn always brings some of her prize-winning pumpkin pies. She keeps them in an ice chest in the back of their truck, and you can have a big slice with cheese or a glob of whipped cream. Take your choice.

There was homemade root beer too, and cider and hand-cranked ice cream, and I haven't even named it all.

Violetta and I were so hungry, and we wanted to try everything. At least I did. I started with root beer and a smoked ham sandwich covered with mustard, and then I just kept right on, winding up with a candied apple.

Except for Sukie, who was probably home still feeling sorry she didn't win, we saw a lot of kids from school. Violetta spotted Roger and the whole soccer team buying sweet corn, and she steered us right on past. I was glad they hadn't seen us.

There was entertainment out in front of the Ford Agency—a four-piece band and a couple of clowns for the little kids. We hung around there for awhile listening and eating.

When Violetta said she wasn't hungry anymore and I was stuffed, we moved on up the street. That's when we saw Roger again. This time there was nobody with him.

"The guys have gone out to Saxon's field to play ball," he said, "but I have to see Doc Willoughby this afternoon. I'm already late."

"How *is* your arm?" asked Violetta

"Okay, I guess. Just boring. Buy hey, your Invisible Man was a winner. And I didn't even know you'd come back."

"Of course you didn't. It was just last night."

"You would have known," I said, "if you'd been home. I called."

"Anyhow," he said, "I'm glad you're here." His face got kind of red. He muttered a good-bye and was gone.

"Poor Roger," I said. "We'll see a lot of him until he gets that cast off. Come on, there's more to look at."

All the stores had special sales and Mrs. Mitchell, who still has her gift shop in spite of the mall, had a table out on the sidewalk—lots of beads and earrings. Mr. Steuben had a table too, with all sorts of stuff—sunglasses and soaps and vitamins and even a rack of paperback books.

It wasn't until we wound up at the other end of Main Street that we found the Judge. Jessie always puts a chair or two out in front, and that's where he was sitting, having a cup of coffee. But he was alone.

"Where's Doff?" I asked.

"She went back to the house. Had some things to do. I said I'd watch for you and we'd be along in a little while. But tell me about the contest. There were any number of potential prizewinners there. I'm glad I wasn't a judge."

When we told him, he congratulated Violetta, and she said, "I wouldn't even have entered if it hadn't been for Amy."

"Speaking of you and Amy," said Grandpa. "I was thinking you might like to go with us tomorrow, Violetta. We're taking Doff to the city, but we'll be back in the evening sometime. It's going to be a little rugged for Amy and I'm sure she'd like to have a friend with her."

I hadn't thought of that and I said, "That's a great idea. Of course she'll come."

"Oh, I'd like to," said Violetta, "but we have to get settled in again, and I think Jessie wants Mother to work tomorrow. I don't think I should be gone all day."

"Whatever you say, of course," said Grandpa. "It's up to you."

But I wasn't going to let it be up to her. "Ask your mother just the same," I said. "She may want to get rid of you."

Violetta laughed. "You might be right."

Grandpa started to get up. "How about right now. I'll come along if you'd like. I want to get another cup of coffee anyhow."

That's when I did some quick thinking, and I said, "No, you stay here, both of you. I'll ask, and I'll get your coffee for you too, Grandpa. It's time you got some service from me."

Grandpa looked a little surprised, but I grabbed his cup and headed for the door. Violetta's mother had never paid any attention to what I had to say. Maybe she wouldn't now, but when I found her and Jessie together at the counter, I just blurted out what I wanted.

While I waited for Mrs. Mills to answer, Jessie jumped right in on my side. "That's peachy," she said. "I intend to keep

Selma busy all day. There will still be crowds around because of the Faire. I'll need her help."

"Violetta can go with us then?" I still looked at Mrs. Mills.

She looked at Jessie and when Jessie grinned and nodded, she looked back at me.

"Yes," she said, "tell Letta yes. It's all right."

It was like she wasn't afraid anymore.

I'd been holding my breath and now I let it out and said, "Well, that's settled, Grandpa needs another cup of coffee."

It was Mrs. Mills who filled the cup, and with a good feeling, I went back outside.

"There you are," I said to Grandpa, putting the coffee down in front of him, "and it's okay. Violetta can go."

I guess I sounded a little smug, but believe me, my good feeling was swept away when I looked across the street and saw Mrs. Jenkins hurrying toward us.

"Judge Ryker," she called out before she even reached the table. "I just heard you're going to be left alone with Amy sooner than you expected."

The Judge said, "That's true. We're losing Doff tomorrow."

"And you still have no one to take her place."

I knew she was getting to that, and I stood there biting my lip.

"That's true too," said Grandpa, "but . . ."

"Well, you just set your mind at ease. I want you to know I am free and will be happy to take over for you."

I was sure Grandpa wouldn't go for this, but I couldn't wait for him to say so.

"Actually," I said, "the Judge and I got along so well while Doff was away last week, I don't think we're going to need anyone." I was afraid to look at Grandpa, but Violetta gave me a nod and her eyes sparkled.

"Nonsense," Mrs. Jenkins snapped. "You're just a child." Then she turned to Grandpa and completely ignored me. "A little child needs guidance and supervision." She sort of clicked her tongue. "And you and I, Judge Ryker, know that men are helpless when it comes to dealing with children. Especially girls."

I think that got to him. Grandpa didn't like Mrs. Jenkins any more than I did, and he said, "Thank you for your offer, Phoebe. We'll let you know if we need you, but there is really no emergency. Amy and I intend to work something out."

I wasn't sure what he meant, but at least he hadn't said I was wrong. I'd just let it alone.

Mrs. Jenkins looked surprised, but she had more to say. "Of course, if you have other arrangements in mind, I wouldn't want to interfere. Just remember, I might not be available when you need me."

"I guess we'll just have to take that chance," said Grandpa politely, "and thank you again."

She went off mumbling, but I didn't let her get too far.

"Mrs. Jenkins," I called after her. "I'm not a little girl. I'll be twelve in December."

We didn't stay too much longer after that. Grandpa finished his coffee, and when Mrs. Mills came out to see if we wanted anything else, he thanked her for letting Violetta go with us to the city. "We'll pick her up about seven-thirty," he said, "if that's all right with you."

She looked over at Violetta and then said, "Oh, yes, and thank you for asking her, Judge. She likes Amy."

Violetta gave me another nod and I said, "We'll see you in the morning."

On the way home I got to thinking about Mrs. Mills. After all, she was Violetta's mother—a different kind of mother maybe—but she was all right. Somehow she didn't seem to trouble me anymore.

XXV

SUNDAY CAME whether I wanted it to or not. We were all up by six, and Doff's bags—only two—were at the front door by the time I came downstairs. We didn't talk much and didn't bother with breakfast. The plan was to have something at Jessie's when we picked up Violetta.

There were two phone calls—one from the president of the church guild to wish Doff a safe trip, and one from Mrs. Enslow reminding her to write. They didn't hold us up, though. Grandpa said we were right on schedule.

At the coffee shop, Mrs. Mills smiled a lot and served us hot cereal and applesauce. When Violetta reminded her that she might be late getting home, it was Mrs. Mills who said not to worry. "We'll be busy here. Jessie says she'll need me until at least ten. You just have a good time."

How about that?

By eight o'clock we were in the car, Doff in front with the Judge, Violetta and me in the back with books and notepads and a bag of cookies. Jessie pressed a little package into Doff's hands and we were off.

It was going to be a long drive and I was sure glad Violetta was with us. If I'd been alone, I would have had nothing to do but think. This way, as soon as we got on the highway we started a game of Twenty Questions.

Doff and the Judge talked away up front, but we didn't pay any attention to their conversation. When we were tired of our game we read awhile.

About eleven-thirty we stopped for lunch at a place Doff spotted along the highway. It was good to get out and stretch, but none of us was very hungry.

Doff opened the present from Jessie, a bottle of perfume—lilac, of course. There was a note.

Newton Grove will miss you. I'll be here for Amy if she wants me.

Doff said, "Jessie is a good person."

"She's neat," I said, "and I'll go see her more than ever now."

"I suppose you will," said Doff. "Your grandfather tells me you and he are going it alone, at least for awhile."

"Amy's idea," said Grandpa. He looked over at me and smiled. I guess we were both remembering Mrs. Jenkins, but he did surprise me. He must really think we'd be all right without anybody.

"I think you'll get along splendidly," said Doff. "Just take good care of each other."

"Well," said Violetta who had been pretty quiet, "Amy says she can manage a can opener, but if she can't I'll show her."

Everybody laughed and Doff said, "Amy's fortunate to have you, Violetta. You girls stick together now."

From there the conversation drifted to Doff's flight, and Violetta wanted to know how long it would take her to get to London.

"About seven hours from New York," she said, "but I'll lose the better part of a day because of the difference in time."

"You'll lose more than that if we don't get you to the city," said Grandpa, and we piled back in the car.

Violetta and I played other games—I Spy and Going to Market. The time passed.

When we finally arrived at the airport, Grandpa let us off at the curb with Doff's luggage, which she was able to check right through to New York. Then we waited while he parked the car and came back to join us.

Violetta had never been to an airport before, and she was excited about everything, the moving platform, the security check, and the long walk to the gate.

The plane was scheduled to leave on time, and Grandpa had figured everything just right. People with children were already boarding when Doff checked in, and it was only a few minutes before they called for the rest of the passengers.

"Well, this is it," he said, taking her hands in his. "I don't like to see you go. Take care of yourself now, and write to us. You know how we feel about you."

"I do indeed," she said. "I'll keep in touch. You are my family." Then she turned to me. "Amy, my dear, I hate to leave you." She hugged me so tight I could hardly breathe, and when she let go her cheeks were wet. I'd never seen Doff cry.

I was numb. This whole day was unreal, happening to someone else. I stood there with no words at all. I just hugged her again, and when there was another boarding call I watched her walk to the gate. She turned, waved a last good-bye, and was gone. Gone.

All at once tears streamed down my face. "I'll come to see you," I called after her. "I promise. And I'll be all right. Just wait and see."

Grandpa put his arm around my shoulder. Violetta moved a little closer to me, and I reached over and took her hand.

F
BRA

AUTHOR
BRADLEY, VIRGINIA

TITLE
WAIT AND SEE

F   BRADLEY, VIRGINIA
BRA   WAIT AND SEE

Quakertown Elementary School
123 S. 7th Street
Quakertown, PA 18951

DEMCO